Praise for LB Gregg's
*Trust Me If You Dare*

"The scenes are that descriptive and the characterization is that well done. Trust Me If You Dare is entertaining as hell, ranging from action-packed to hilarious to sizzling hot."

~ *Joyfully Reviewed*

"The dialogue is witty and full of non-stop quips and jokes. It's never overwhelming or too over the top... LB Gregg has a definite flair for comic timing and anyone looking for a light hearted, delightful romp won't be disappointed."

~ *Whipped Cream Reviews*

# Look for these titles by
# *LB Gregg*

*Now Available:*

*Romano and Albright*
Catch Me If You Can
Trust Me If You Dare

# Trust Me If You Dare

*LB Gregg*

Samhain Publishing, Ltd.
11821 Mason Montgomery Road, 4B
Cincinnati, OH 45249
www.samhainpublishing.com

Trust Me If You Dare

Print ISBN: 978-1-60928-310-0
Digital ISBN: 978-1-60928-268-4

Editing by Sasha Knight
Cover by Mandy M. Roth



First Samhain Publishing, Ltd. electronic publication: December 2010
First Samhain Publishing, Ltd. print publication: November 2011

# Dedication

To my dear friend Tracy.

And a special thanks to my pal Hank.

# Chapter One:
# Cappy's

Approximately four point eight seconds prior to impact, Tommy Cappelletti spat the raw edge of his mustache from the side of his mouth and said, "The first thing you need to know about the 328i? It's touchy. You hear what I'm sayin', Caesar? The accelerator is probably more responsive than what you're used to." He gave me a sideways look. "She'll go zero to sixty in under four point eight seconds. So go ahead. Tap it."

*Tap.*

The word seemed innocent enough, but this kind of manly camaraderie isn't really my thing, and I swear he was throwing down the gauntlet. Subtly challenging my masculinity from the relative safety of his passenger seat. His cowboy hat was cocked, his mustache drooped, and he seemed slyer than your average car salesman. When he winked, I couldn't stop myself from tapping the gas with a stomp. How fast could this thing go in reverse anyway?

Gravel flew, tires squealed and we pealed out with far more enthusiasm than the Pish Posh Nosh delivery van had ever shown. Before my foot could even touch the brake, I was thrown into my seat belt. A nauseating *crunch* filled the plush interior of the car.

I'd never hit another vehicle in my life, but that sound was unmistakable. We'd—*I'd*—cleared the parking space and crossed the driveway in under...well in under four point eight seconds. "Shit."

"Holy fucking shit," Tommy agreed, clutching his seat belt with a chubby hand. His wedding ring was imbedded on a sausage-thick finger, and his limp string tie draped his knuckles. He whipped around and stared bug-eyed at me. "Did you...? Did you just? Did you...?"

I found some comfort in his stuttering, as I'm afflicted with the same tendency. "I...think...yes...I..."

An alarm binged from somewhere inside the car—there was an astonishing array of whistles and bells and all of them seemed to ring at once. On the video screen, the backup camera's dotted red line indicated *stop.* I had stopped, all right—stopped on the bumper of another Beemer. Thank God the airbag hadn't deployed.

"I...I...I am so sorry. I'm...I'm not much of a driver. I may have mentioned that?" I shouldn't be behind the wheel at all. I should be watching the dealership. Watching in case someone walked in. Someone whose photo Dan had handed me fifteen minutes earlier—a slender redhead with a splash of freckles across her nose. She looked twelve. I was at Cappy's doing a favor for my new boyfriend, PI and former NYC Detective, Dan Green Albright. He said, *Text me if she shows up.* However, with no viable excuse for loitering in the empty showroom, a desperate car salesman had appropriated me.

"*Holy Christ.*" Tommy Cappelletti's panic was on the rise. He sucked half his mustache in on a breath and blew it back out. With the stutter, the low-riding cowboy hat and the long, bushy brows—and those now-bulging eyes in his flaming red face—the man was a dead ringer for Yosemite Sam. "You hit that car." With a click he freed himself from the seat belt, his mustache flaring like bellows. The metal seat belt buckle clacked against the passenger window as he tossed the strap from his waist and gripped the door handle. "What did you do?"

"Well, I...I...didn't realize the car was so fast in reverse. I drive a delivery van and you have to wrestle the gas pedal. You said *tap* and I thought you meant *punch*."

"If I meant punch it, I would have said punch!" Tommy hollered as if somehow his anger could change the recent course of events. I was still immobilized by the accident. He was flailing and furious. "I told you it was responsive. What did you think that meant?" His pallor shifted from pale to ruddy and back again. Did he have high blood pressure? He was flashing like a neon sign.

"Let me move forward an inch so we can see the damage." I gathered my wits and, grinding the gears until I found first, I released the clutch and jabbed the accelerator as Tommy fell from the open car door.

The door slammed. Tommy sprang to his feet, jaw swinging open again.

*Pop!* I jerked against the seat belt and everything went white. The airbag exploded from the steering column and smacked my chest like a fucking two by four. Stars. Lights. Pain. My top tooth pierced my bottom lip and the acrid scent of chemicals filled my nose.

I punched the airbag away and sucked oxygen into my lungs. It took only a few tries.

What the hell was I doing in this deathtrap German car? It was filled with fog and I had an airbag deflating on my lap. White particles floated around me. Another first. I'd never seen an airbag explode. There was a dull ringing in my ears and my face felt funny. In the rearview mirror I could see a bright spot of blood welling on my lower lip. I licked it, the taste a mix of tin and salt. Maybe it was baking powder. Although, who knew what that white powder really was? For all I knew, it was anthrax.

The crumpled hood of the car gleamed at me through the windshield. I'd bounced off a large silver sedan. *750Li* read the chunky silver letters on the now-crooked trunk of the car in front of me. BMW. Zero to sixty held new meaning for me and, as Dan would probably add later, I was unsafe at any speed.

I unbuckled and searched the door for the handle, feeling for the latch or lever or bar that would free me from this nightmare.

A massive palm slapped the window next to my nose—as if I wasn't scared enough?—and I reared back.

Outside the car, an angry young man with a five o'clock shadow at nine in the morning glared through the window. I hadn't seen him before, because I would have remembered the pugnacious jaw, the equally prominent brow and the bleached buzz cut. He looked like he'd recently escaped from tenure on death row. His green coveralls named him Stew. His tattoo was homage to his mother. His arms were huge and his reach was flipping long—those knuckles nearly scraped the asphalt.

For some reason, call it *self-preservation*, I sat put and swiped at my lip with the heel of my hand. The smoky interior of the car might be carcinogenic, but I could deal with that. I looked at Stew and my mind registered *immediate threat*. Therefore, I settled back in my seat, airbag on my lap, no hurry to move. Stew could hurt me far worse than the two consecutive fender benders combined. I wiped my lip again, this time with my finger. It came away bright with blood.

"Get out of the car." Stew rattled the door handle, but I was safely locked in. Tiny flecks of his spittle sprayed the glass.

"Open the door, asshole, you're bleeding on the upholstery."

Right. Did he think I was stupid? Not that I'd given him any reason to think otherwise.

Ignoring Stew, I rattled through my *what to do in the event of a car accident* list.

*Remain with the vehicle.* Check. The spittle flecking the driver's side window ensured that I wasn't going anywhere.

*Exchange insurance information.* Insurance? Yosemite Sam should have asked me for a card or something before I got in. He'd been so eager, bordering on desperate—luxury car sales must be down—and he hadn't asked to see my license. I was at fault, but in a court of law, who was responsible? We were still on the lot. I should probably call an attorney, or my cousin Joey who was studying to become an attorney.

I licked at my lip and stared at the row of buttons on the door. There were eight. Which was overkill, in my opinion. Why did they need so many? The van had one button, a crank for the window and a handle to open the door. Simple enough for the most reluctant driver. Dan's bike required nothing more than a leg over the seat and hanging on for dear life.

*Dan.* Where was he? Was I dazed? My ears clanged, chalky dust coated my hands, and it hurt to breathe. How hard had that fucking airbag hit me?

Employees in sport coats and polo shirts wandered the dealership. They joined the cowboy-hat-wearing Tommy Cappelletti. The growing group fanned in a horseshoe, staring goggle-eyed at the car. Periodically, they'd squint through the privacy glass to check me out—talking or pointing and shaking their heads.

*Call law enforcement.* That one was tricky. I sighed, prepared to call the only law enforcement I knew. I wouldn't be in this mess if *Detective* Dan Albright had dropped me off at work in the first place, which had been the plan prior to a phone call he'd received minutes after we'd engaged in some scalding hot sex in the shower this morning. My thighs were still sore from that stunt he pulled with the shower rod.

Dan was somewhere inside the dealership meeting with a suspiciously attractive man from the service department—I bet it was the same man who called us five minutes post coital. We'd been a block from Cappy's Luxury Auto Sales when he gave me that funny hitched smile of his—the one that made my chest a little too tight—and said in a way sure to get a rise out of me, "This might take a few minutes, baby. Try not to break anything."

Break anything? At the time I'd responded with a huffy, "I don't know what you mean."

Which was our way. He liked to yank my tail, and I pretended to dislike it.

We'd walked into Cappy's and Dan ditched me. He'd sauntered to the service desk, his leather jacket over his shoulder, his smile crooked—those brown eyes steadfast on a blue-collar blond. The two men shook hands and then they slipped from view.

I'd ground my teeth and waited. Watching the door vigilantly and pretending to flip through a slick catalog of dangerously fast cars—and secretly hoping to eavesdrop on Dan's covert conversation with the smiling, strapping mechanic—when Tommy literally latched onto me. The overzealous car salesman seized my elbow and steered me outside. I had to hand it to him, he was good. He smooth-talked me, hypnotized me with his silver-tipped cowboy boots and dreams of freedom on the open road. It had all been a fine distraction...and the entire lot was visible from there. If the girl in the photo arrived, I'd have seen her—I mean her hair was the color of cayenne pepper. Impossible to miss.

A beefy hand slapped the glass again and I, brave lad, located my cell phone.

"You need to open the door!" the big man yelled.

I held up my index finger. "Just a sec. I need to make sure I don't have whiplash." I pretended to roll my neck—which *was* a little stiff—and watched Tommy through the rearview mirror as he stared mournfully at the back end of the car. Regret washed his features.

It couldn't be *that* bad.

The thug outside the window stepped in front of the car. A crowd followed him. The front bumper had to be worse than the back.

What would my father do in this situation? He'd open the sunroof and let the chemical gas out. I should do that. I found the button on the roof console and let the sunroof open a scant inch. New York City air wasn't exactly a clean exchange, but at least my eyes stopped tearing.

I speed-dialed Dan with my thumb as a row of jaunty, colorful beach balls swayed in the summer breeze. Each ball was speared by a thin metal rod. They lined the sidewalk cheerfully—I guess they were supposed to resemble festive balloons there to beckon would-be car buyers onto the lot. *Come and see what we've got.*

Dan answered his phone, that deep voice resonating over the line. "Romano? Where are you? There's something going on outside."

"Yeah. That would be me. Where are you? You're taking a long time." I would not be jealous or suspicious. He was working on a new case. He was Dan Green Albright and the warmth in his voice reminded me that I trusted him.

"John did me a favor. We're almost done, but you should call Poppy and tell her you're running a half hour behind. I know you two are busy."

"I think I'll be running later than that..."

"Give me five. I'll buy you a donut."

That sounded promising. "Sure..." Stalling. I was stalling with a deflated airbag in my lap, a bloody lip and a minor blow to the sternum. "But I want one with the cream on the inside."

"You do, huh? So what's going on out there?"

"I... See... You were taking so long...I..."

"Shit. What happened?"

I took a breath and choked on the air in the car.

He barked, "What? Did someone get hurt?" I pictured him morphing into cop mode, glaring through the plate-glass window of the car dealership ready to take names and issue warnings.

"Not yet." Although Stew was seething on the tarmac. "I've had an accident. I was test-driving a car."

There was a muffled cough.

I wiped my lip again. The blood had stopped. "You should probably help me before the locals remember where they keep the torches and pitchforks."

"Sit tight. I'll be right there."

"Will do. I'm not leaving the car."

Tommy knocked on the driver's window, his hat mashed in one freckled hand. His string tie was undone and so was he. His forehead glistened in the morning humidity. He said very loudly through clenched teeth, "Mr...."

And then he paused.

Tommy sucked on his mustache and slid a look to his

fellow employees. They waited expectantly. And waited. Waited until it became patently obvious to everyone on the lot that Tommy had failed to get my full name before allowing me to drive a forty-five thousand dollar car. I felt marginally better, although goddamn it, I was still mortified.

My cell phone vibrated with a text message from my business partner and best friend, Poppy McNamara.

*Do you think the pickles-and-ice-cream thing is true? Can you stop at Guss' on the way in? Get me one of those big pickles. We have an appt at 11.*

Tommy knocked on the glass again. "Caesar. If you would please step from the vehicle, we need to assess the damage. No one's going to harm you."

Not harm me? Why the hell would he even mention that? The thug at the front of the car met my stare. His eyes were flat. He rolled his neck and shoulders, cracked his knuckles, and nodded.

Screw this. I started the car.

It took three tries before I realized starting wasn't an option. Tommy said with wire-thin patience, "You can't turn the car on after the airbag deploys. It's a BMW."

"Well, that's not helpful at all. I'll just wait here for the police, thanks. Can I still use the battery?"

He nodded.

"You said this has satellite radio? Does it have OnStar? How about air?"

"Mr. Caesar, we don't need to call the police. Let's get a copy of your license and check with your insurance company." His Adam's apple bobbed. "You are a licensed driver, aren't you?"

"The name is Romano, and of course I am." It was even

valid, although only just. Poppy kept nagging me to go down to the DMV—damn thing still had my folks' address listed. I found my aged license in my wallet, rolled the window down an inch and slid it to Tommy. "Here you go."

He seized it. His gaze flickered between the photo and my face. He worked his mustache again, asking with a hint of disbelief, "This is you?"

It was a bad photo, true. From seven years ago, back when my hair was long and I'd worn it combed to the side. There was also the sparse mustache. What can I say? I was young. At the time, I thought I resembled a dashing young Valentino with my dark eyes and sleek hair—and all the encouragement from my ex, the now-famous TV star, Sheppard McNamara.

The thug sauntered over and took my license from Tommy. "You look like Father Guido Sarducci." And then he did the most unsettling thing. He fed his meaty fingers into the gap I'd left open in the window. His hands came in to the third knuckle, and he wriggled his squat fingers at me. "Open the door, asshole."

What was taking Dan so long? It was a tiny lot, for fuck's sake. "Calm down and get your goddamn hands away from me."

I hit the door lock as my phone rang. "Yeah?" There was a crunch and a scream from outside and then the tough guy's fingers vibrated against the glass. His fingers were stuck, that idiot. I jabbed all the buttons on the door. Nothing happened, although the door locks popped—

It was Dan. "Caesar, what the hell—"

The tough guy's voice was pinched and high. "Open the window! Open the fucking window!"

I hit the window again, this time locking the door. These damn buttons weren't intuitive. "I think it's stuck!" I pushed on the thick neck's fingers and he blubbered, so I let go. Why the hell couldn't I open the window? "Just pull them out!"

Tommy Cappelletti yelled, "You have to press start. Press start!" He banged on the glass.

The start button was the only thing in the entire vehicle that made any sense—although not currently because it didn't start the damn car. I drew a breath deep into my lungs. There had to be twenty-five people standing around me, some of them in suits, others dressed in shirts with their names stitched above their breast pockets—not one of them named Dan Albright. All of them yelling advice. I was getting pissed. Correction. I was royally pissed. "Get your fucking hand out of the window, asshole."

I found the button and the window slid down another half inch. Pale fingers disappeared, and I snapped that bastard closed as quickly as possible while Stew doubled over, hand in his crotch.

I hung up on Dan, who stood with his cell phone to his ear, the hot, buff blond beside him at the edge of the crowd. I gazed through the sunroof, although there was no help coming from above. So I did what any self-respecting Italian kid from Brooklyn does when they're in a bind: I called my cousin Joey—the attorney to be—to find out if I needed legal counsel.

Ten minutes later Dan and I headed toward his bike, which was parked at the mini-market on the opposite side of the street from the car dealership. We left the pandemonium at Cappy's behind us. The morning was moving swiftly along, much like Dan running from the scene of my accident—*accidents*. His long legs ate the crosswalk and I quick stepped to keep pace, my face sweaty, my lip puffy, my pride wrinkled. I shook my hair and white powder spotted my work shirt like dandruff.

It would be a stretch, but I'd just pretend this morning—from the time we arrived on the lot until this very minute—had never happened.

Although forgetting was difficult with the evidence of my recent disaster directly at our backs.

Muscle-necked Stew had vanished, which was excellent news. I lost sight of him while Dan calmed Tommy enough to coax me from the vehicle. Unfortunately Tommy Cappelletti was seated behind the wall of glass in the manager's office—hat in thick-fingered hand—getting what looked like a stern reprimand by Cappy himself. Cappy was a tough customer in a well-cut banker suit and a pricy pinky ring. His calfskin shoes were butter soft and scuff-less—mob shoes.

Obviously we were hightailing it the fuck out of there.

"Slow down." I had a stitch in my side, and something told me that the pain was going to increase upon the arrival of my next insurance bill.

Dan didn't slow, but he turned to offer me a wink and a smile. His teeth were white in the morning sunshine—and his grin was filled with good humor, which I hoped wasn't at my expense. He looked cool, calm and collected. I admire that in a person. "C'mon. Let's get a cup of coffee. You look like you could use one. I know I could."

"I'm fine." Which was a white lie. I kept a lid on the subject of my sore ribs, because this shit always seemed to happen when Dan was only one step away. Usually my life was uneventful. "I just want to go to work. Let's take a rain check on the coffee and you can drop me off at Posh Nosh." I checked my watch again. "Tick tock."

"Hey. I'm not the one who held us up." Dan's composure finally broke and he choked on a laugh.

"Problem?"

He shook his head and tried to cover his amusement with a poorly executed cough. His broad shoulders shook, and I narrowed my eyes. "Do you need me to smack you on the back—?" I left off *of your head*, but it was clear I'd do that.

"No-no. I'm good. Just wondering how in the hell you managed to hit both cars."

I held up a hand. "Don't say another word, I'm embarrassed enough. Let's just get out of here."

"What about the donut?" He looked between the mini-mart and me. "You love donuts."

"I'll pass. I should get to work. You're finished here, right? Did you find the redhead?"

He shook his head and unhooked his helmet from the back of the bike. "Nope. I have someone keeping an eye on the place." He didn't need to say who—the blond. "If she was here, she's gone now. You weren't exactly discreet."

"She must be timid."

"Not really."

"Sorry." I clicked my own hot helmet on my possibly anthrax-encrusted hair and waited for Dan to start the bike. "Tomorrow, it would be better if you drop me off before you start detecting—or I can take the ferry."

A strange expression flickered across his face—as if he had something to tell me but was weighing every option. It's not a look I appreciate—though I'd seen this one before. Maybe it was presumptuous of me to expect to spend the night again. We were new at this relationship, tentatively feeling our way into each other's life; maybe I overstepped. I was about to ask him, but the Harley's engine roared to life and Dan said over the noise, "Let's roll," so I slung a leg over the bike and grabbed on.

# Chapter Two:
# Piece of Cake

Half hour later I was behind the counter at Pish Posh Nosh with bigger fish to fry.

*Cocktails with Sheppard McNamara*

*Actor*

*16 June 6 p.m.*

"You can*not* be serious." I tossed Shep's invitation on the counter as Poppy nodded anxiously. Her platinum hair fell pin straight and neat to her shoulders. Her signature headband today was ebony satin dotted with tiny smiling ladybugs. Cute. She'd just confirmed that we were onboard to serve drinks to my long time ex and his fawning actor entourage day after tomorrow and I hadn't known. That was unprecedented. Poppy occasionally kept secrets, but this was different. This was business.

I touched my lip and hid a wince. My chest was definitely bruised, I had chemical dust in my hair, but I was at work. Romanos were tough stock. And my insurance premium was about to skyrocket. Best be prepared by earning some dough. "Shep sent these to his *friends* to have drinks in his own home?

He says *actor*. As if they don't already know? He's so—"

"Pretentious? Egomaniacal? Vapid?"

"I was going to say clueless...but yeah. All of the above."

"It's *Shep*. No duh. This is part of his self-promotion package. He needs exposure for that soap award and the new show. He's gotta win the heart of America or some crap like that. I said yes to this as a favor and, I'm sorry, I know neither of us wants to do it—he's a jackass—but it's too late to back out." She squirmed on her stool.

I filled another napkin holder on the lunch counter and snapped the lid. "It's not that it's Shep." We'd come to a sort of mutual understanding recently. "It's that I don't understand why you said *yes* with such short notice. Two days? Are you nuts? We have too many events scheduled—and you told me specifically that we'd take Friday off." I wasn't just bitching. We'd catered one gig or another nonstop for the last six weeks—not to mention keeping the lunch counter running, the bills to pay and recovering from the spring disaster. "I have plans." Dan and I were going to Westchester for my first parental meeting. Six weeks we'd been together and his parents were still a mystery to me because, honestly? I was hesitant to take this next step in our relationship.

A little more than hesitant—I'd actually cancelled three times.

She said, "I said don't plan anything—and you told the entire staff we're closed. What the fuck, Ce?"

"I thought that's what you meant when you put big black *X's* on the calendar."

"I meant the weekend was reserved." She sniffed. "I wanted to do something special."

I spun the invitation with my index finger. It was ebony, high gloss and embossed with a gold martini glass and a silly top hat and cane. My uncle Tino had a printing business in Brooklyn, among other side interests of questionable legality, and having worked in and out of the art world for years, I knew quality invitations when I saw them. I didn't expect anything less from Shep. "Liar. Shep sprang this on you last minute and you didn't have the heart to say no."

Poppy bit her lip and concentrated on icing a genoise cake with a narrow metal spatula. She spread chocolate ganache along the perimeter, delicate white disappearing under a thick layer of cocoa brown. Raspberries peeped between the layers and my stomach gurgled. I should have had that donut.

Poppy ignored my never-ending quest for sweets. She hedged. "See. This is why I need you. I was going to handle the party by myself, because I knew you wouldn't want to be involved...so yesterday I agreed, because what kind of caterer would I be to lose a Friday-in-June gig? And then Shep called last night and asked me to come as a guest."

I dropped everything, including my jaw. "Are you kidding me? Why?"

"I'm his cousin? I don't know, but I bought a dress this morning."

That was news. Poppy was stylish, but frugal. "You bought something *new*?"

She nodded, not meeting my eye. "Sort of. Joey knows someone and he got it for me at cost from Bergdorf's. It's red. Shoes too."

"That was fast."

"I had to move on it."

She was starting to sound less like a Connecticut prep and more like a penny-pinching Romano by the day. "So now you want me to serve alone?"

"It's small—I think he said thirty tops. I've made most of the arrangements. I want to go as a guest. He invited me—"

I held up a hand to stop her prattling excuses. "To an *actor* event? You? I mean, not that there's anything wrong with other actors"—surely there were some reasonably sincere actors out there. Somewhere—"but this is Shep. He hooked up with your former boyfriend."

"Jean Luc was not a boyfriend. He was a *fuck you, Daddy* date for brunch at the club. That's all."

"That still doesn't explain—"

Poppy slapped the spatula into the bowl. "Fine. It's because I feel shitty, all right? He feels sorry for me because I'm huge and fat and waddly—"

"You're hardly waddly. And I don't think it's Shep feeling sorry for you."

She flipped me off.

"I hate to ruin your pity party, but you've only gained six pounds."

"I'm four months along. I've gained substantially more than six pounds." She rubbed her little rounded belly. She looked like she'd swallowed a grapefruit. Otherwise she could pass for a member of the New York City ballet.

"You cannot be serious. You're going as a guest along with Jean Luc Pappineau and Shep's miserable agent, Estelle Rosenstein, because you're hormonal?"

"I know, but...Shep's invite extends to the Soapies." She worked thick frosting, turning the plate with smooth economy—and she steadfastly avoided eye contact with me. Her best friend. "The whole effing enchilada. I want to go!"

"Soapies."

"The award weekend."

"Two days? A two-day orgy of minor celebrity? And we're not earning a single dollar? You can't be serious. Soapies? Good Christ, Poppy, what the hell were you thinking?" I imagined half-dressed starlets and fit, firm Ken dolls smiling toothily for the cameras. Fit. Firm. Tan. Dan would have something swell to say about this.

"Shep is paying. Just...he's paying under the table."

"Well, that's at least something."

"And...the tickets were free," Poppy said as if that made all the difference in the world. She wiggled in her chair. Her legs were crossed and her black flat flapped as she jiggled her tiny foot at warp speed. Her baby bump stretched a few polka dots on her knit skirt. She made quick work of the cake, then lingered, nibbling on a finger full of frosting. There was a touch of hesitancy in her voice. "Well. You know...there's this show I follow when I go home at night...Joey's always studying or working...and the actor from *Days* will be there. He's signing autographs." She lost her dreamy look and said staunchly, "I'll hand out business cards, of course. Posh Nosh should expand into larger venues. We need the income."

Poppy's cheeks pinked and I blinked a few times at this new incarnation of my hardboiled, potty-mouthed partner. Under my perusal, glowing pink skin flushed fire-engine red, a red as startling as her blouse and the tiny ladybugs on her headband. This had to be pregnancy-induced behavior, right? Poppy blushing? I grabbed the next napkin holder, shoved paper inside and shut the box with a snap. "If we need the income, which we do, you shouldn't have taken the weekend off and closed the shop."

"We'll be open during the day—I've got it covered. And I'm not going to work until I'm dead. I need a life."

I wasn't listening, I was lecturing. "And you aren't a soap

opera fan—you're crushing on some...some...Backstreet Boy of daytime."

With an eye roll, my real Poppy returned. "How fucking old are you? Backstreet Boy? I just think it'll be fun, okay? I never go anywhere unless I'm wearing an apron. And neither do you. It's kind of exciting. Otherwise I'd tell Shep to stick that queer invitation up his ass."

"But not the tickets to the Soapies because suddenly you're a gushing fan?"

Her eyes narrowed. "Fan? That's a strong word, Romano. I'm being supportive."

"Right. Of whom?"

She handed me the chocolate-covered spatula. "Mind your lip."

My lip was puffy, but chocolate was chocolate.

Poppy's smile was saccharine sweet. "I'm supportive of my cousin, of course. Shep recently came out to the media as a flaming homo, and he needs his friends and family by his side during this trying time."

"Oh, please. He's fine. He's cashing in. I can't believe you expect me to pick up a tray and serve pot stickers to my ex-lover, his TV friends and his ghastly new boyfriend."

"I know. Believe me, *I know*. I'm sorry but...all the waiters booked elsewhere. I cannot imagine why. Oh wait. That's right. This is your fault."

"No. I'm left holding the bag so you can stalk some non-English-speaking actor."

She nodded unapologetically. "That too. He's not just any actor—have you seen this man? Gunter Heidelbach. He's tasty."

"Stalker. Of course I've seen him. He does those tear-jerker commercials for animal rescue."

"It's so tragic—he's heartbroken over the plight of puppies."

"It's PR."

"That's harsh."

"You need a twelve-step program."

"And you're bitter. You need to lighten up."

"I'm sure he likes puppies very much."

"Please, Ce? Please, please, please? It's just Friday night. I have the lunch counter covered by Andre and Jason. We're not closed; we're resting. I'll make it up to you. Promise. And, guess what? I have a surprise for you."

"I don't like surprises." I said sourly, "We should be catering this entire event for the Soapies. That's the league we want to play in. We're still recouping our losses from that debacle with Rachel."

"Don't start. She's in jail. We're moving on. New York City Nights is catering the Soapies. I tried to land that gig months ago. I did!"

"Sure you did."

She threw her napkin at my head, and it hurt to dodge a damn piece of paper. That devil airbag had tried to kill me.

I went into the kitchen to find a Perrier and a couple aspirin. "What's Joey have to say about this?"

"Here's the best part. He wants to know if you'll be my date. He has to study."

Oh, I just bet he did. I was going to have words with my cousin.

"He said to tell you that he wanted to go because it's an open bar with free dinner, but he can't."

"I have free dinner all the time. My father owns a restaurant. And, newsflash, we're caterers." I perched on my stool and started filling salt and pepper shakers, but my curiosity outweighed my bitchiness and I found myself asking, "Date for what exactly?"

"The awards ceremony. You'll need a tux—I think Joey has something you can borrow, but it's blue. Vintage. I'm wearing red both nights—we should coordinate—although maybe red, white and blue isn't a good idea? It doesn't matter. We make a beautiful couple."

"This is your good news?"

And even though I knew better than to be flattered when Poppy buttered me up so sloppily, I had to give her her due. Technically, she was right. We *were* striking. Like a perfectly matched bride and groom topping any wedding cake in America. Petite Poppy with her silver hair and gamine blue eyes and me, Italian dark, swarthy and slim. She had a tiny frame and a tall attitude—we were proportionate. But no matter how attractive we'd be dressed to the nines as guests at a black-tie affair hosted by my rich, handsome and famous ex—instead of dressed in our usual drab catering attire—I shouldn't be swayed. Damn her.

I knew I'd do it anyway.

I said again, with emphasis, "Dan and I have *plans.*"

"Liar. I bet he's working and you're taking Nana to the market. So what? You'll have sex with your boyfriend this weekend. Big deal. Whoop-di-do."

It was a big deal, by the way. A very big, hot, orgasmic deal that I enjoyed enthusiastically and athletically, thank you very much. After years of drought, I had a lot of catching up to do in the hot-sex-with-well-hung-new-boyfriend department.

Poppy ranted, "You can come with me and still have sex with Dan later. Don't be a party pooper. We'll have fun and I'll be your designated driver. You can get bombed on champagne.

You can flirt like a man whore and pose as Shep's mysterious and handsome ex."

"Are you high?" I'd need to be to sit through an entire evening with Sheppard in his newfound Out/Proud Actor role. I was happy for him, sure, but he was cashing in on his sexuality and I found that...distasteful. Why did it not sit well with me? "I'm not a pooper. I'm spending time with my boyfriend."

"Oh whatever. Get a grip. Live a little."

And that was that. Because Poppy McNamara wasn't the first person to say *live a little* to me recently. I had to be the most conservative queer in New York City. I hadn't been to a club or party or bar in years.

I didn't even know any drag queens.

I filled shakers and considered the invitation while Poppy prepped another cake. This one had pear filling and cinnamon-cream frosting. She smacked my hand with the spatula when I tried to pinch a nibble. With a sigh, I relented. "If I do this, you owe me. You owe me big."

"Oh, what else is new? Plus I love you and you love me. This is how relationships work."

"If you say so." But she was right. "I love you too. Yes, of course I'll go."

Poppy slopped some frosting on a raspberry and handed it to me. "Go uptown and see what Shep wants for this thing."

I choked on the berry and rasped, "Go *where*? To Shep's? Does it not occur to you that this scenario is getting worse not better? Why? Why can't he come here, or do this over the phone, like every other client in New York?"

"Stop crying, Ce. Because he can't. I'll frost a cake for you. Special. Please? He's expecting me at eleven, but I have to go to the gynecologist."

That stopped me cold. I wouldn't ever argue with the word gynecologist. I could scarcely say it out loud. There were some things I was better off not knowing.

"Don't make that face. It's just the gyno. You're such a fucking Guido sometimes..."

"Fine. I'll do it. For the record, this is under duress. I've had a strenuous morning."

"I know. Poor thing. You're puffy and sore and poor. I love you anyway."

"Right. I want Mocha. Mocha frosting and no fruit. Chocolate cake—nothing fancy with green tea or spices. Lots of chocolate cake. Multi-layered. And sprinkles. You may write *All hail* on the top."

"Deal. I'll sparkle that bitch." Poppy handed me my messenger bag, my cell phone and my favorite mineral water. She gave me a packet of M&M's for the ride. She bullied me to the front door of Pish Posh Nosh, all hundred six pounds of her, and flipped the sign from *closed* to *open*. "Go. Find out. Time is tight. He waited until the last frickin' minute. We have shit to do."

I rolled my eyes and searched my bag for my bus pass.

Poppy chattered, "And you'll have so much fun with me this weekend. You'll see. It'll be like old times. We'll get fancy and hit on the gay men."

"I'm in a relationship," I said primly. "And so are you."

"Well. We're not dead, Caesar. We're just going to have a little fun."

I glanced at her swelling baby belly, and she slammed the door in my face. *Touchy*.

On the street, it was already sweltering at midmorning. So far, I'd had shower sex, destroyed three cars, pissed off a hard-working man named Stew, and I, along with my now-dented ego, was heading to my ex-boyfriend's to offer my free services as his personal fucking caterer.

The day was off to an auspicious start.

4th Street was clogged with street vendors, trash cans, tourists, students, businessmen and vagrants. Some broiling idiot in a soiled chicken suit passed me. I dodged and scurried as horns blasted. Truck exhaust filled the air.

I crossed the street. I had to take the bus uptown to Shep's luscious apartment—and for once, I wouldn't make a fool of myself while I was there. Cool as a cucumber. That was my new motto. Suave. Sophisticated. Employed.

At least for the rest of the day.

I drank my bottled water, winced and waited for the bus.

# Chapter Three: Coffee and Cigarettes

Uptown, a bevy of photographers were camped in front of Shep's discreet building on 57th Street.

They hadn't been here six weeks ago.

Shep must be orgasmic over the attention. The paparazzi loitered without shame, resting against the iron railing, waiting for someone noteworthy or newsworthy. Since I was neither, I marched along the sidewalk cloaked in anonymity. These chuckleheads must be hoping for a lucrative shot of Sheppard—Mr. Daily News. His dream come true. However, when the photographers marked my presence with raised camera lenses, I was unnerved. I tried to ignore them, but it was hard once the cameras started clicking.

The inattentive doorman let me in with a slack wave. Security wasn't any tighter, with the exception of a newly installed high-tech security camera that faced the elevator. Was it just for show or was the doorman monitoring the building?

When I was four feet from Shep's apartment, my phone vibrated. Alone in the barren corridor and reluctant to proceed further into Shep's sphere, I took the call. I could be a minute or two late. It wasn't like I was paid extra for punctuality. I leaned next to a potted fern and found a beam of natural light filtering in from the large window at the end of the corridor.

It was Dan. "Hey."

"Hey yourself. How's your lip?"

"Puffy. Did you find the redhead?"

"Nope. Still looking. What are you up to?"

"Work," I said evasively. "Poppy has me checking out a gig." I was embarrassed to admit exactly what else I was up to this morning. Working for Shep was a blow to my dignity. "You...uhm...wouldn't believe me if I told you."

"After Cappy's this morning, I'll believe anything you tell me." He was right. Still, he'd have a lewd comment remembering our first visit to Shep's apartment—which had ended with the two of us getting it on under the guest bed after we broke in and were nearly caught. Frantic, blistering hot, impressively fast sex on the bedroom floor, hidden beneath the bed skirt. Our first time together. It had been excellent, of course, but if that's all I could think about before I even walked through the door—Dan nailing me to a three-second, underwear-ruining climax—this job was going to be more difficult than I realized.

Shep's apartment now equated sex with Dan. My personal happy place. I had to keep my thoughts clean and lust-free.

Right.

"Caesar? Hey. Are you there?"

"Sorry. Where are you?"

"Pretty much the same—you wouldn't believe me if I told you. I'll fill you in later. You want to grab lunch?"

"I *am* starving..." All that chocolate frosting had triggered my appetite. My watch said eleven. "Why don't I meet you at one? You can pick the place—or we can eat at the shop."

"Sounds good. I have a few people to check in with."

"Yeah. Me too, actually. I'll call you later." I pocketed my phone and forced myself to knock on the apartment door. Poppy needed me. She was my best friend and, if the shoe were on the other foot, nothing would prevent her from meddling in my life.

I waited for the door to open, psyching myself for the job. I was a professional businessman. I could do this, no sweat. It beat working in the Stuhlmann Gallery any day—although, weirdly, I couldn't shake either Shep or Jean Luc since that night at the gallery six weeks ago.

The door snapped wide and I put on my game face. It was lost on the prissy stranger who greeted me. He was three inches shorter than me, making him officially *short*, with black hair and vibrantly blue eyes and a shave so close he seemed nearly prepubescent. His hair was stiff with product and his skin weirdly devoid of pores, smooth as a baby's bottom. He wore a leopard-print ascot and matching pocket square, which was off-putting. He seemed vaguely familiar, but I couldn't place him. He certainly wasn't Shep's type. Jean Luc was large and in charge and liked it rough. Shep and this guy together? They wouldn't know which end was up. I figured him for a stylist or a hairdresser, like one of those *What Not To Wear* people. He could easily pass as Clinton Kelly's little, very little, brother.

He said grandly, "May I help you?"

"I'm here to see Shep." Had he moved? I looked over the man's head into the apartment. Behind the twink the foyer was empty, but music drifted down the hall. Muzak. It was like standing inside an elevator. Clean and serene, and about what I'd come to expect from this apartment.

I'd been here twice before and it was an impressive piece of real estate. What it lacked in *joie de vivre*, it made up for in sheer breathtaking expense. Shep had taken two large apartments—even by non-New York City standards—and joined them into one whopping living space. His kitchen was nearly the size of Posh Nosh. No kidding. His living room had a fireplace and a partial view and had been dressed by an interior decorator with all the verve of a Pottery Barn catalog. What a waste.

Although, at age twenty-eight, I still didn't have a place of my own—so who was I to judge? I'd paid off some of my towering debt with the reward money I'd earned a few weeks ago, but I was living in Nana's guestroom and I couldn't see my way clear of it. The arrangement worked, though a little solitude and privacy would go a long—a very long—way for a single guy in his late twenties. Plus, I was tired of traveling to Staten Island for a nooner.

"He's indisposed. Do you have an appointment? You're not his eleven o'clock." The dapper young man tapped the screen of his iPhone and a whiff of cigarette smoke hit my nose. That was strange. Dan sometimes smoked when he was working. I'd come to associate the lighter scent of tobacco with his presence. "Perhaps we could pencil something in for next week?"

"I'm expected."

"And you are?"

His slow perusal of my work threads was condescending at best. There was nothing wrong with my jeans. I was hip, young and...okay, I had a canvas messenger bag slung across my bruised chest, not quite *GQ*, but I was working. And I'd die before I wore a leopard-print pocket square.

The youngster's gaze landed on my swollen lip, and I said regally, "Tell him that Caesar is here."

"I'm sorry but your name isn't on the calendar." He scrolled and tapped a beat with his thumb on the phone.

A plinking rendition of "Endless Love" underscored our strained conversation as I retrieved my own phone. I texted one

McNamara, Sheppard. *I'm here for our meeting. Your doorman won't let me in.*

Twink smiled kindly. "I'll tell him you stopped by." His attempt to close the door was foiled by my foot. I stepped into his personal space, crowding my way into the apartment—a technique I'd learned from Dan, who had all kinds of tricks up his sleeve.

"I didn't catch your name. You're the new doorman?"

He bristled. "Stephen Taylor. I'm Mr. McNamara's personal assistant." Stephen did not offer his pale hand. I knew this game. I'd been a gallery assistant for years. He said crisply, "And you are Caesar *who*?"

"Caesar!" Shep slid into the foyer on bare feet, a towel hastily secured around his lean hips. Water beaded his freshly manscaped chest. With flushed skin and sopping hair, he was still better looking than the pre-bearded, under-forty Brad Pitt, only blonder. It irked me that years ago I'd been hoodwinked by Shep's boyish face. I learned the hard way that Shep's best assets were appreciated when the lights were off and his pants were down.

Shep held his phone. Bewilderment and remorse and something like panic made his voice crack. "Oh my God. I'm so sorry." His gaze flitted between Stephen, the back hall and me.

Stephen murmured, "Oh. I see. You're the *caterer.* You should have said. Come in. Mr. McNamara said you were his cousin. I expected someone...taller."

For the record I'm five foot ten in my best shoes.

Unfortunately, those were at home in my closet.

Before I gave Stephen the dressing-down he deserved, Shep said, "Poppy called and said she had to go to the doctor, so I thought she cancelled. I didn't think—"

"You didn't think that I'd come. I almost didn't, but we only have two days. Let's get cracking." I opened my bag and searched for my notebook. "I hope all you plan to serve is liquor and have a few floral arrangements or we're screwed. Poppy has appetizers covered, but I have no staff. Why don't you get dressed and then we can discuss logistics." An eerie deja vu made my skin crawl. It wasn't the first time I'd had to wait for Sheppard to find his clothing so we could solve a problem. He might be perfectly comfortable wandering around buck naked, but I wasn't in the mood for his exhibitionism.

Stephen shut the door and we lingered in the spacious foyer. The hardwood floor gleamed, the papered linen walls were cleanly elegant, and Shep dripped on the Persian rug with panache. A fifteen thousand dollar Jean Luc Pappineau sculpture—a bust of Shep as new conservative TV hero Mr. Potter—stood on a table by the kitchen door. Why was I not surprised?

"Right. Pants. I should do that." Shep seemed strangely fascinated with the front door, and then he glanced worriedly into his spacious living room.

"I'll prepare the study." Stephen sighed as if he were readying a room for a war tribunal. "That's probably safest."

Safest? I clicked my pen uncertainly as Stephen exited.

Shep babbled, "Drinks. For the party, I mean. That's all we need. Just a few cocktails. Champagne, of course. We can put a bar in the dining room. Some light snacks. I expect fifty people, maybe seventy. Eighty on the outside."

My pen stopped clicking. "Eighty guests? *Here?* Are you insane? Where are you going to fit all those people? Is there a balcony? Although room capacity is the least of our worries..." Why had I given all twelve waiters the weekend off? Where was I going to find a bartender at such short notice? Poppy would have to tie an apron over her knock-off dress and fling canapés at the celebrities herself. *Shit.* "Shep. This is definitely a problem."

There was a knock on the door. Instead of answering it, my host shifted his towel and leaned nonchalantly against the wall. He didn't bat a lash and those caramel-colored eyes widened innocently.

I sucked my teeth because I'd seen this show before. He was hiding something.

The knocking continued.

I smiled. "So. Do you want me to get that?"

He glanced over his shoulder again.

"What are you hiding, Sheppard?"

He sighed. "Promise me you won't freak, but I scheduled another appointment."

"Why should I care? You double booked and then took a shower instead of dealing with your obligations. That seems predictably well thought. Your assistant is really earning his keep." That was bitchy but my ribs hurt and, no surprise, I wanted to wrap this meeting and move on. We had only two days. "Don't you think now would be a good time to locate some pants? Unless this is the impression you're hoping to make." I was like a broken record, but he wasn't following my refrain.

Stephen scooted in from the study. He breezed by me to answer the door. Another task that used to fall to me when I worked in the gallery. His job was thankless, I knew. I'd have to remember to treat him with kindness.

Shep backed away saying quickly, "Maybe you could wait in the other room?"

"You're trying to get rid of me? Fine."

I was about to leave when a deep voice I knew far too well

asked, “He here?”

The assistant prattled happily, “You must be Mr. Albright. There’s been a mix-up with our appointments this morning. The caterer showed after all.”

I blinked at Dan. He must have called me from the lobby. “What are you doing here? I thought you were seeing someone about a job?”

“I am.”

“So am I.”

Dan stepped inside the entryway and his presence made the room snugly intimate. Tall, dark and broad-shouldered, he had no trouble commanding a room when he chose to. He looked the same as he had earlier, dark-washed jeans and motorcycle boots, but now his mirrored sunglasses were tucked in the neck of his shirt.

His focus zoomed in on the cushy blue towel covering Shep’s privates. Dan kept his mouth shut, miraculous as that may seem, while Shep made soothing sounds and wet the carpet. Stephen rambled on about shifting appointments. For a second, I swear he took my photo with his iPhone. Dan listened to the assistant and leaned in to give me a quick kiss, avoiding my swollen lip. His warm mouth brushed mine and my lips tingled.

I responded to his friendly gesture by stiffening up, prissy as usual. He smelled like coffee and chewing gum and something...odd. Something sour. Something that had me taking a teensy step backwards.

Dan gave me a knowing smile—clearly he thought I was uncomfortable over the PDA. Which was often the case. I could never tell if he kissed me in public to stake some kind of claim, which was nice but unnecessary, or simply because he was more comfortable with his sexuality than any man I’d ever slept with. He just did as he pleased. It was refreshing and a little frightening.

He asked, "What are you doing here?"

"Poppy roped me into something. I was going to tell you over lunch." I needed to tell him that meeting with his parents was out. I'd do that over lunch as well. I was racking up the cancellations, and food might ease his disappointment.

"Okay." Dan nodded toward our nude host. "Why's Shep naked?"

Shep said nervously, "I just had a shower."

"All right then." Dan said, his friendliness suspect, "Just so you know, *Mac*, people attend business meetings with their pants on."

I sighed. "I told him as much."

"Did you now?" Dan wasn't as blasé as he acted. He was annoyed. He'd shown amazing restraint in the past with Shep. He glanced down the hallway. "Is he here yet?"

Shep's gaze flickered toward the back hall for the umpteenth time. "Yeah. He's getting dressed."

My eyebrows hit my hairline. Did he have a naked man tucked in the back room who was not Jean Luc Pappineau? *No way.*

Shep added lamely, "I was about to get some pants." But he made no move to do so. Instead, he fumbled to enlighten me. "I asked Dan to stop by. Estelle thinks I need help handling the security situation on Friday. A professional. You know? A hired gun and—"

"Like Clint Eastwood?"

Dan snorted. "Careful, Romano."

Shep continued with his story, "Just in case there's a problem. The photographers, the reporters, some of the fans—

they can be persistent. After the thing with Jean Luc, when I made the announcement—well, when my publicist made the announcement—everything changed."

"When you came out, you mean? You can just say you're gay. We know. We're all on the same page."

He didn't say it, but he did nod. "I'm not playing Detective Dan on *Days* anymore, and I'm not the Wheaties guy. I'm that *gay actor.* And with the new show, the ratings are surprising—"

Blah. Blah. Blah. I knew. His new show, *Mr. Potter's Lullaby*, had every GLBT organization in America seething. The first episode had been an epic nod to homophobic Middle America—missionary Potter had ridden into an Appalachian hill town to spread the gospel of Traditional Family Values. It had spiraled ever downward from there. Shep did look good as a missionary. I had a feeling men and women all over the country tuned in weekly just to see him in shiny cowboy boots and ass-clinging jeans.

"—and then the daytime award nomination and all these social obligations, Estelle suggested I hire someone to create a security plan."

"That would be me." Dan's deep voice drowned the Muzak. "At least for the weekend."

"How cozy." I smiled.

Dan winked. "You bet. My hourly rate for this sort of work is steep."

"No kidding, right?" Shep said.

Stephen, whom I had forgotten, possibly because I couldn't see him standing behind Dan, said, "Mr. Albright, may I introduce you to...the caterer."

Shep said testily, "Are you retarded? They just made out. Go get us all some drinks or something." He wiped his forehead with a palm. "He's new. Sorry. Estelle sent him over."

Dan opened the door to the hall. "You two have your meeting. Tell Gun I'll be here at two fifteen. He's not to step a foot out the door." He placed a small black box on the hall table. It looked like a TV remote. "Give this to your roomie—it's a GPS tracking device—we removed it from the car."

Shep's eyes went round. He backed away like the GPS was armed and dangerous. "Why the hell—"

"I turned it off." Dan shot a look my way. I couldn't tell if he didn't want to have this conversation in my presence, making me the official third wheel, or if he was keeping something from Shep. Dan said to him, "I'll go over the details with Gun later."

"That sounds ominous," I said and feigned a shiver as Shep's lips thinned.

"Very funny," he said.

"Nah. It's standard. I'll be the hired gun." Dan winked, the big goof, then added to Shep, "But only for the weekend, and then, if you're serious about security, time to hire the big boys full time. You're going to need people to travel back and forth to L.A. with you. I can give you some referrals."

Shep clasped his towel. "That sounds expensive."

"It's the price of fame." Dan glanced down the hallway one last time, "Two fifteen," he said. He gave me a nod—which I interpreted as *Shep's an asshole, but cash knows no enemies, please don't start with me*—and he let himself out the door.

Shep sighed. "Let me just go find some pants."

"Probably a good idea." I followed Stephen into the study and waited to meet the mystery guest.

Shep disappeared into the back bedroom and I was left to entertain myself on a floral settee in a sunny room behind the kitchen. Bookshelves lined the buttercup-yellow wall. Fresh organic coffee steamed in a rose-patterned bone-china teapot. A spread of delicate cups, moist lemon squares and fragile doilies graced the coffee table. It was like visiting Poppy's parents in Connecticut. I guess Shep was taking his entrée into the sisterhood more seriously than I thought.

I put three sugars in my coffee, stuffed an entire lemon square into my mouth and waited. The treat was tart, buttery, sweet and...I wanted a second one. I stuffed another in my mouth and daintily brushed confectioner's sugar from my jeans.

Stephen puffed a sigh of disgust at my lack of manners and handed me a *People* magazine before he left to conquer some thrilling assistant's task. I chewed vigorously and read the titles on the bookshelf. It didn't appear that any of the bindings had been cracked.

I was alone for less than a minute when Gunter Heidelbach, soap star and puppy-loving spokesperson, strolled into the room wearing deconstructed jeans and a pink Johnny Cupcakes T-shirt. I lost my grip on my cup and the coffee splashed the saucer. I don't know what I expected, but it wasn't that he'd show up here to speak with me. Poppy would have shit a brick if she knew Gunter was sequestered in her cousin's cushy apartment just off Park Avenue. She'd have knocked me down and come for this appointment herself. Served her right. I nearly texted a quick, *Neener neener, you loser*, because here was her obsession in the flesh.

I had to admit at this close proximity I could well appreciate her interest.

Gunter Heidelbach wasn't your typical buffed and polished Hollywood actor—like our host, who was still finding trousers somewhere down the hall. Gunter was spare but broad shouldered, rough with a sparse morning beard that I found distressingly masculine. He held an unlit cigarette tight between two fingers and his dirty blond hair was slick from the shower. His feet were bare and tan. He had the polar opposite appeal of Shep McNamara—and in a way, he reminded me of Dan.

Until he opened his mouth.

"Hullo, *Liebling*. You ah my bodyguard? I am Gunter, but you will call me Gun, yes? It will be your job to keep my body guarded this weekend. Very lucky job for you, right?" He grinned, unrepentant of his own conceit. "But, Sheppard didn't warn me you were attractive. Do you jujitsu?"

What the hell could I say with my mouth crammed full of lemon squares? I swallowed and stood to shake his hand, not knowing what else to do. Gunter took my outstretched hand carefully, trapping it inappropriately between his, while, wide-eyed, I choked down the rest of my treat. I pulled to withdraw from his grip, and his smile deepened and his hold tightened. He had unsettling apple-green eyes framed by laugh lines, and I was as caught by his gaze as I was by his hands.

Dude was strong.

He smiled broadly. "You're too slight to be a bodyguard. Are you Shep's?"

I licked my sugary lips and found my voice. "No, I'm the caterer. I've come about the party." I wrestled free from his clutches. "I'm not slight. I'm average height."

"Oh. I know you now. I saw you on the Internet. You ah the ex."

"Internet? No. I'm sure you're mistaken." I didn't cop to the ex. I sat on my end of the sofa, steadfastly ignoring the temptation of a third lemon square, and waited for the ex.

The plate of dessert beckoned. Maybe just one more...

Gunter plopped down beside me on the couch, tucked a foot under his tight butt and twisted around to offer me the brilliance of his full attention. Startled, I leaned back into the arm of the couch. Gun's eyes sparkled. "You ah Caesar Romano, the roommate and the first luff. The secret college lovah. Three years. You ah a mystery—Shep has been discreet, if you can belief that." He chuckled and I was concerned. What had Shep said? "But he let some things slip and thus, I just read about you."

"About me? Why?"

"Because Shep is a curiosity—making the big show of his sensitivity and homosexuality just in time for the awards, I think. He's shoplifting my niche. I need to know to whom I am against, and so, I researched. Also it's very dull here this morning. His apartment lacks zest."

"Well, you're pretty well-known, don't you think? Lots of airtime lately. With the puppies. And kittens."

"Yes. This is the case." He took a lemon square and placed it in my palm, then carefully licked confectioner's sugar from his fingertips, his eyes locked on mine. His tongue was very red. I squirmed a little. What the hell was with this guy? He was really too much. "My life has become a media circus, and so I must be careful."

"Surely it's not that bad."

"It is. Some scandals ah worse than others."

Gunter's accent was flavored with Germanic undertones and clipped, but only enough to make him sound exotic, not entirely foreign. I expected him to speak like Colonel Klink, since that's how he came across on Poppy's soap. He was about my age, late twenties, but he'd lived a little. He didn't look concerned about anything today. He seemed more interested in flirting—but he was an actor, he could be hiding murderous intent behind a charming smile while selling you toothpaste and cracker snacks. Actors were not to be trusted.

I glanced at Gun and he stared with ill-concealed longing (an act, surely) at a spot just above my lip. I wiped my face with a floral napkin and winced when I grazed the split.

Gun chatted, spilling beans happily. "As for me? I am hiding from the press in this boring apartment until after the weekend, and then I leaf for California. Now I cannot go outside without some sort of ruse. Baseball hat and sunglasses. Not even to have a cigarette."

"You're hiding here? I thought..." I thought nothing, actually. If Dan was working for Gun—and he was—well, he usually kept the details of his job hidden under his own ball cap. Which was fine by me. But...I was intrigued. Was Dan protecting Gun? Digging for dirt or concealing it? This would be the topic du jour over lunch. Gun watched me closely and I said, "I thought you were Shep's new lover showering in the back bedroom."

"I didn't say I wasn't, luff." He winked and the crinkles deepened around his eyes. He lifted his unlit cigarette to his mouth and frowned. "Damn."

"Don't listen to him, Ce," Shep announced from the doorway. "Gun is crashing here for a few days while his apartment is being painted."

I rolled my eyes. "Please. I've known you for ten years. You're too sincere to be telling the truth. The man is hiding. He said as much."

Shep tried for funny. "Nah. He's too cheap to stay in a hotel."

Gun leaned in to whisper, "I'm loaded. I make him look like a shoeshine. Don't listen to *him*." His hand crept toward me on the back of the sofa. He lazily caressed the fabric, slowly encroaching on my personal space. I stuck a chintz pillow between us and gave him my most quelling look.

Shep poured a cup of coffee from the china pot. "Gun, you moron. You're not supposed to... Okay fine. The truth. But only because Gun can't follow the simplest instructions—"

He flopped against the seat. "*I am bored.* I am lonely. I cannot even step onto the balcony to smoke one fucking cigarette. It makes me crabby. We have a guest, you should be happy to have your handsome ex-lover offer help to you. You are very lucky and completely unappreciative." Gunter smiled at me and moved infinitesimally closer. "He doesn't deserve you."

"Well, that was always the case..."

Shep snapped, "We're taking you somewhere later. Can you behave yourself for one goddamn minute? This is serious."

Gunter smiled roguishly at me. "You may join us for the outing."

"I'm already out, thanks."

"Oh for fuck's sake, Gun. Give it a rest."

How novel to see Shep exasperated by the behavior of someone else for a change. While it was both interesting and entertaining, I had work to do. I put my cup on the table. "So—about Friday."

Shep turned to me. "You can't tell anyone Gun's here until Friday night. Not Poppy, not anyone. Do not tell Nana."

"I thought you said he was having the apartment painted? What's the big deal?"

"It's. Complicated. Just don't say anything. I can't...handle it right now. I can't even tell Jean Luc."

Gun smirked and reached for his cup. "That man is a douche."

"I've mentioned that on occasion." Jean Luc Pappineau was

a shit. He had once taken Poppy to the club for a lunch date, and mid-meal he excused himself to go jerk Shep off in the men's room.

Shep ignored the douche exchange, stating, "Here's the deal. Jean Luc is out of town, so Gun and I will host the cocktail party on Friday, with appropriate PR spin and media handlers. Sixty to seventy guests, a few reporters, strict security and lots of booze—but none for Gun. Make a note somewhere, Ce. No booze for Heidelbach."

"You take away all the fun." Gun sucked on his unlit smoke.

"I'll get Stephen to handle the details. You keep the booze flowing and the food coming. Thematically, I'd like something black tie and gold trim."

"Reminiscent of the Oscars," I said with a straight face. "Check."

"Oh. Exactly. Can you do that in two days? You did a great job at Papp's opening in April. I mean, before I was drugged, assaulted and the gallery was robbed."

"That wasn't my fault."

Gunter assessed me, "You ah an interesting man, Caesar Romano. Dare I say naughty?"

"No. I'm neither interesting nor am I naughty. I'm a caterer. So full bar, passed hors d'oeuvres, and a baby sitter for the talent," I said as Gun pouted beside me. "We'll handle everything except security."

"That's what your boyfriend is for," Shep said.

"Boyfriend?" The talent sighed in dismay.

That was my cue to leave. I grabbed my messenger bag and headed for the exit. "I'll come by tomorrow and show you what I have. Two days, Shep. I hope Poppy's charging you double."

"Triple."

I smiled. "That'll do."

Outside, the full row of paparazzi trained their massive lenses on me for the first time in my life. They must have done some digging while I was enjoying my lemon square. I did my best to ignore them. A couple shutters clicked before, one by one, they got what they needed—which seemed to be photos of me doing my deer-in-the-headlights impersonation—and they settled back to watch the door. My first time in the media storm, and I looked sweaty, puffy and mediocre.

One man broke apart from his the herd and approached me, leading with his outstretched hand, which I avoided. He had that heterosexual male combination I would never understand—bald crown, two-foot ponytail. He was very chummy as he said, "Hey. You're Caesar Romano, right? You're McNamara's ex."

My feet stuck to the pavement like I'd sunk ankle-deep into bubblegum. I was getting a little tired of hearing that. Since I was the one who broke it off years ago, by rights he was *my* ex. Really, these reporters should get their facts straight. I searched the street for a quick exit and moved my feet accordingly.

The intrepid reporter followed close behind. "I did some research on you."

"Not very exciting, I'm sure." Last time I'd been Googled a measly fifteen items popped up. That was six weeks ago when Dan had investigated me—which was how we met, actually. If Gunter was correct, maybe it was time to do another search. Maybe Shep had done the kiss-and-tell after all. Not that it mattered. There wasn't a person of my acquaintance who didn't know I was gay. It wasn't something I could have ever hidden, and was as much a part of me as breathing, or being Italian. I simply didn't care to have my photo splashed all over the internet. I didn't want my poor judgment in college to get mentioned in the gossip rags.

Particularly if I looked sweaty and swollen.

The photographer persisted with his false overture of friendship. "I'm Jorge. Jorge Carrera." His smile was all teeth. I reluctantly shook his hand. He was slimy, and so was his hand. "Not exciting? I think you have a good story. Do you have a minute?"

"Story? Not right now. I...I...uh...have a...lunch date."

"With Shep?" He handed me a business card, which I didn't take. Apparently long practiced in the brush-off, Jorge Carrera was unperturbed. "I'm hoping to get an interview, maybe find some new insights to your former relationship with Shep McNamara. You know, during the closet years."

I choked on something that tasted like...astonishment. Me? Interview?

Jorge continued, "I'd love any comments about his current romantic ties."

"I *really* have nothing to say." What could I say that Jean Luc and Shep hadn't already? They'd snogged on live television. Jean Luc had the bad grace to manhandle his own nipple piercing during polite conversation, and he enjoyed displays of public ass grabbing. Those photos were worth a thousand of my words, easily.

"I understand he and Jean Pappineau are on the rocks."

"I wouldn't know. I'm a caterer, not Dear Abby."

Carrera pounced. "So you're catering an event? Is that here? Does it coincide with the Soapies? How does it feel to work for your former lover? Is it awkward? Who is on the guest list?" Jorge followed me down the sidewalk yakking and asking impertinent questions while I searched my messenger bag for a roll of Tums. If God loved me at all, Jorge would fall into an open manhole. Carrera was pissing me off, and his monstrous camera kept knocking into my arm. He asked slyly, "I heard that Mac and Gunter Heidelbach were sighted together."

"Gunter who?" Maybe the reporter would quote me and Gunter would crap a *nobody loves me* monkey, but I thought I covered for those two admirably.

My phone chirped. Jorge pretended not to look at my phone's display. "Excuse me."

It was Dan texting to say he was waiting for me on the next block. Halle-frickin-lujah.

Jorge banged my arm again with his overtly phallic telephoto lens, and my messenger bag flipped—I managed to catch my laptop, securely held by its Velcro straps, before everything else hit the fucking sidewalk. I usually carried my messenger bag over my chest, but it had irritated my blossoming bruise. Papers, my notebook, pens, my stash of Life Savers and my emergency M&M's were all now strewn across the filthy pavement. The forgotten photo of the redhead—the same one Dan handed me earlier—fluttered to the ground. "Shit."

"Oh, I'm so sorry!" He didn't sound sorry. He was either palsied, or he'd hit me on purpose.

Jorge bent to snag the photo and his too-inquisitive eyes met mine. "Schmidt. Kendal Schmidt. That's an odd photo to carry around. You know her?"

"No." But apparently the photographer did.

"This is Gunter Heidelbach's personal assistant," he said slowly, as if I were an idiot.

"Right-o." Why was Dan looking for Gunter's assistant? I snatched the picture from Jorge's sleazy hand and shoved my crap back into the compartments without bothering to organize any of it. I said with all the politeness I could muster, "That's *fascinating*. If you'll excuse me? I really want...er...*need* to go."

His look was too insightful by far. "Sure. We can talk while we walk. Where are you headed?"

"I have a thing."

"Oh. Right. If you want to talk, I promise to handle our interview with discretion. I can arrange compensation for your time."

"No, thank you." *Buzz off. Fuck you.* That's what I should have said, but getting quoted in the *Daily News* wasn't high on my to-do list. And besides, Nana would make me put a quarter in her cuss jar.

Jorge retreated. I waited in the smog for the light to change as the photographer headed into the alley toward the side entrance of Shep's apartment building. He was crafty and shifty and more intrepid than he let on. I wasn't going to have to keep my big secret about Gunter's hiding place for long. The entire world would know the second that good-looking German snuck through the side door with his false mustache and his poorly chosen beard (Sheppard McNamara) to grab a smoke in the alley.

Gun was effectively a prisoner of the apartment. Those two would probably kill each other, if they didn't fuck each other first.

# Chapter Four: Peeping and Lurking

Halfway down the pedestrian-clogged block—exactly as promised—Dan Albright waited for me. He leaned against an unfamiliar white Toyota Camry, head bent, dark hair falling across his forehead. He needed a trim to keep his cop look up to date. His biceps bulged in the navy T-shirt clinging to his sculpted body. He fooled with his BlackBerry. Mirrored sunglasses hid his eyes.

I was hot, I was hungry, the ache in my left side had grown into a pronounced throb, the city was filthy with the sweat of a million commuters, and I was sure an unflattering photo of me would appear in tomorrow's gossip section. Therefore, despite his appeal, or perhaps because of it, I bordered on snappish when I joined him. "So what's the deal, Albright?"

"With Shep? 'Bout what he said. It's a security gig for the weekend. That's all." He barely glanced my way, pocketing his phone with a practiced move. He retrieved a set of keys from the snug front pocket of his jeans. The Camry beeped and its locks clicked.

I stared at the car. I'd never seen it before. "Funny you didn't mention this job earlier. Like this morning over breakfast or at any point last night."

"It's no big deal."

"When were you going to tell me?"

"I was going to tell you last night, but—"

"But you didn't want me to know."

He finally looked my way and my own dark eyes reflected back at me. "I wasn't hiding it, but I knew you'd be like this. I was just waiting for the right time to tell you. It's only a couple of days. I don't want to fight."

"I'm not fighting."

"Ce. You either trust this thing or you don't."

"You mean us? Of course I trust this thing. That's a little passive aggressive of you," I said. Dan held the car door open, which was always a surprise—I could open a damn door by myself. "It's Shep and that Gunter Heidelb—" and then I got a whiff of the interior. "Holy shit." My eyes watered. "What is that?"

"Massaman Chicken Curry, I think. Someone left a takeout container in the backseat and it spilled. It baked in here overnight."

"*That's* why you smell. You can't be serious. I'm not riding in there. It smells like feet."

"I know. Believe me—I had to drive this thing over here. I just need to get some air freshener."

"You're going to need more than air freshener. You're going to need a different car." I stalled. "Whose car is this anyway?"

"I'm using it for surveillance." He was smooth, I'll give him that.

"You're going to sit in this car, in the heat? All afternoon? With bad chicken? That's a health hazard."

"I threw the chicken out. It's fine. Just get in."

"And don't think I didn't notice your non-answer. This belongs to the mechanic from Cappy's, right?"

"Look at you, Mr. Junior Detective." He took one step forward, close enough to enter my personal space, and smile in place, he brushed his mouth against mine. That dimple appeared.

He was trying to soften me up. While I was charmed by his effort, and anything but soft now, I was not amused.

"Don't get that look. Just get in the car, Romano. We can grab lunch. Please." I started to say something, but his grin stopped me. He wasn't movie star beautiful; he was rugged and full lipped and forty. His nose was bold. The lines around his eyes were deepening. He had a scar on his lip and a jaw that was never smooth of whiskers. I looked at Dan and all I wanted to do was let him take me away.

Only not in that car.

"C'mon. You can put a hankie over your delicate nose and then you can fill me in on what Shep and Gunter had to say, because I have work to do. And so do you."

"I do. Can you believe this? Two days to prep for seventy people."

"Sounds exactly like him. C'mon. Hop to, baby. Get in the car."

I didn't want to. Jesus. I'd rather take the bus. I stalled, "When did you start working for Gunter?"

"Yesterday. Shit you not. Estelle and Shep gave him my number."

"He's a gay Casanova." Apple-green eyes. Fit, funny and worldly. I flung my hands in the air to make a caustic comment about soap opera stars, but the pungent stench of last night's chicken made me wheeze. Wheezing made my lung throb beneath the fast-growing bruise on my rib cage.

I zipped my lip and waited for Dan to keep talking. He stared back at me, his face inscrutable. I wished I could see his eyes. Gunter and Dan alone, working together. I imagined Gunter's bold hand streaking across the flowery couch to fondle Dan's earlobe and Dan grinning roguishly back.

He walked around to the driver's side door. "He hired me to do some snooping."

I squashed my doubt. "The redhead? The photographer said she's Gun's secretary."

"Kendal Schmidt. She disappeared."

"She's missing?"

"Maybe. I'm checking it out. She threatened Gunter over the weekend and hasn't been seen since. He believes he's at risk."

"From a secretary?"

"It's not unheard of."

He was right. Poppy's former assistant had given us all a run for our money. "If Gun thinks he's in danger, then he should go to the police, or he should leave town. That seems simple enough."

"It's never that simple. He has an image to maintain. He's rebounding from one scandal."

"Scandal? What? Did he come out? Like Shep? That appears to have launched Shep. Apparently, gay is quite trendy."

"No. He solicited a police officer. He's got to be here. He's trying to salvage his career, Ce." His words resonated over the top of the Camry. We both had careers we were nursing along. Dan's new venture as an investigator-for-hire had depleted his resources, and my recent employment with Poppy McNamara and Pish Posh Nosh put me solidly at square one. "Gun's paying me enough money, based on his agent Estelle Rosenstein's recommendation, to make this worth my while. It's the kind of work I want to do—the kind I used to do. Bigger jobs could come from this. I want this."

"Then I want it too."

Dan gave me a crisp nod. "Good. We're on the same page. Let's go, those photographers are still taking your picture."

"What? Why?" Sure enough, from a block away, those parasites had their lenses trained on me. I'd delayed getting in the car long enough. "Fine. For the record, I'm not eating in the car."

"Noted." There was a smile in that word—I heard it. I got in, and Dan rolled the windows down and sighed theatrically. "I guess this means a quickie in the backseat is out of the question."

I snorted. "At least until the car airs out."

The smell wasn't too bad once we were moving, but there just wasn't going to be a fresh breeze in the Camry. Driving in Manhattan you don't pick up enough speed to get any cross ventilation. Driving is a series of fits and starts and limited forward progress—like everything else in my life until recently.

At the first light, I was gasping from the fetid odor of sour meat. "I can't go back to work smelling like a health-code violation. Doesn't the car have air?"

"Trust me. It's worse."

"That's not possible."

Dan snapped his gum and hit the air-conditioning button.

"Okay, okay."

He seemed pretty satisfied when he asked, "So what do you think of Gunter?"

"Gunter. I'm not sure that I trust him. He's too good-looking, he's smooth, and..." Gun's manicured hand streaking across the sofa would replay in my mind all day. "Honestly, I think he just made a pass at me."

"Why wouldn't he hit on you? You're feisty, good-looking and hung."

"I won't argue with that."

Light beamed off his mirrored glasses as he gave me the slow smile that made my toes curl. "I make passes at you all the time and you never complain."

"That's entirely different."

It was, wasn't it? We were exclusive. We had a good thing going—new. Fresh. We were a couple, not that Dan said more than *my ass is yours for as long as you want it.* He wasn't exactly a walking Hallmark card, but then again, neither was I. Far from it.

Dan's tone was cautious. "I need to tell you one more thing."

"Now that really does sound ominous."

"Heidelbach is paying me to spend the night. He says he doesn't trust anyone else, and I need the dough. I'll be camped at Shep's. With those two—a big slumber party. Which means, no sexcapades in Staten Island until this is over."

"Until you find Kendal? What if it takes years?"

"Estelle's going to find him a bodyguard—this is temporary."

I was hardly listening. I was still stuck on the bombshell that *he was sleeping there.* Not just staying there, but Gun was actually paying him to sleep over. It sounded...illicit. He'd been arrested once for soliciting a police officer...how was this any different?

I bit back every word that threatened to fly from my mouth, determined to be the supportive boyfriend of a private investigator. Of course, if he were any kind of detective, he'd have detected a note of anxiety in my falsely calm, "We'll figure something out."

But he took my words at face value. He reached over and squeezed my knee. "Yeah?"

"Maybe. If you're good."

"I'm always good, Romano."

I'll say.

He let go of my knee, both hands now on the wheel at a safe ten and two position. "So. Tell me what Shep and Gunter said."

"Not much. I'm not to tell anyone that Gun's there. Do I really need to keep this from Poppy? She's going to find out soon enough."

"For now. Try. That's all I'm asking."

That would be hard. I'm historically not good with secrets—and I'm worse with lies. In fact, I hate them and, more than anything else, deception causes me to stumble. It's a clear tell that my closest friends and family recognize instantly. "So do you believe Gunter? That he's in danger, I mean?"

"We pulled the GPS off his car this morning. His BlackBerry was bugged. I didn't believe him yesterday—I figured he was high-strung or wanted a PI as a PR thing—but now, yeah, someone's keeping tabs on him. Could be the press. Could be Kendal. Could be someone else."

"So you don't know?"

"No. He's bunking with Shep. No one will ever think to look for him there."

"I don't know, that reporter already thinks something is

fishy."

"He was probably just digging—but I'll check him out." Dan put his blinker on to take the Hudson River Parkway. The river was pea green in the thick of summer.

Cautiously I asked, "What do you think of Gunter?"

"Think of him? He's a client and an actor. I just hope his checks don't bounce."

"I meant about the case."

"Oh. He's right—someone is looking for him. Whether or not he's in physical danger remains to be seen."

"Well, Shep looked like he wanted to strangle him..."

Dan nodded. "Shep has his hands full now."

I mulled on that, reiterating, "If Gunter is in danger, then he should leave town. I, for one, would like him to leave town."

"He's not going to until after the award ceremony."

"Did he speak with the police?"

"Yes, and there's nothing they can do—other than stop by Kendal's apartment and do a welfare check. From what I can tell, she doesn't want to be found and there's zero evidence of foul play."

"What does that mean? She's missing or she's hiding?"

"Hiding. Her boyfriend is unaccounted for as well."

"Maybe they eloped."

He shook his head. "If Schmidt is up to something, Gun will need me to verify that he's being stalked—so when he does go to the police, he has evidence. I agreed to find Schmidt." He glanced at me. I must be wearing my discomfort plainly—I didn't like this—and he was holding something back. "Don't get that look, Caesar. It's a lot of fucking money."

"If he's as solvent as he says."

"His deposit was good. And someone *is* stalking him."

The towering buildings of midtown grew shorter and the streets tighter as we drove into the Village. We came to a stop at the light on 7$^{th}$ and Dan gave me that look—the one that made me feel like we were in this for the long haul. The one that said he valued my opinion and that I was important to him. "Seriously, what was your impression of Heidelbach?"

"He's a charmer. I thought he was bored and that he's going to sneak out of the apartment for a smoke if you're not careful. He's a little spoiled and a little needy, and Shep isn't his favorite person. They bickered and if I didn't know any better, I'd think they want to jump each other's bones."

"That I'd like to see. Except the disappearing-for-a-smoke part. He's too afraid to leave the apartment."

"Today. Give him a couple days. What's the history with Kendal?"

"He fired her. Schmidt's lover made a pass at Gun and when she found out, she threatened him—physically."

"Is she...tough?" I'd fought with a woman before. It hadn't been pleasant. "He didn't file charges?"

"He's worried about his image. He needs to keep his nose clean."

"Yeah, and his hands to himself. I'm glad I'm not his manager."

"You're right about one thing."

"Just one?" I smiled sweetly.

"Correction. Many things. But, yeah, Gunter's a Casanova."

Dan maneuvered the Camry through the rabbit warren of one-way and cobbled cut-thru streets that laced the Village. The place had character—a sense of community that was lost in upper Manhattan's towering buildings and anonymous crowds.

The well-preserved architecture and the artistic flair of the residents—there was always something going on here. It was vital. Vibrant. The Village could be confusing to tourists and was a constant source of frustration to cab drivers, but I loved it. It felt like home.

I relaxed into the seat, my nose pointed toward the fresh air flowing through the open window.

We passed ethnic restaurants, a few cheery coffee shops and the old mom-n-pop groceries. We were five minutes from Posh Nosh when Dan's deep voice pulled me from my musings.

"Do you have a couple minutes? I want to check something quick before we grab lunch." He flipped the blinker with a scarred hand and made a hard left onto Waverly. What I knew about those scars crisscrossing his knuckles and streaking his chest was nearly nothing. There'd been a fire a few years back, and afterward he'd left the force and received a settlement. He was mum about the details, and I wasn't going to press him for more than he was willing to give. I figured someday he'd trust me enough to tell me.

"Sure. Fine." I didn't mind. Poppy had the counter covered, and other than the fact that I had *an entire gig to put together in forty-eight hours, no staff, and no booze*, I had nothing pressing to do. "Anything to get out of this car."

"I promise to make it fast. I know you have a lot going on."

"So. Where are we going?"

"To Kendal's apartment."

"Here?" I gaped. "Wow. Someone has a hefty allowance." Squat, painted-brick-faced historic buildings lined the streets. Here and there a painted stoop or lacquered front door welcomed visitors. Charming green awnings sprouted from some of the doorways. Geraniums and tomato plants grew in clay pots on the fire escapes, thriving in the heat-thick air.

Apartments and co-ops were plentiful—for those who could afford the pricey rent on a single room. I'd lived here once—fresh from college and starry-eyed over the possibility of finding a good job and starting a new life. That dream hadn't quite panned out.

"From what I dug up last night, she found a great deal. And Gun paid her well."

"No roommate?"

"Nope. No pets, no family in New York, although her mother is in Brentwood."

He snapped his gum and I tried not to stare at him. He always knew everyone's secrets. Sometimes his job as a professional snoop made me uncomfortable.

Dan parallel parked into an improbably convenient space, and I exited the car before the wheels stopped turning. I waited on the sidewalk, leaving my bag in the car to give my sore ribs a rest.

He joined me and we headed toward the gray stoop of a four-story brick townhouse. It was squished between two taller buildings. A glass front door and a tiny intercom system were the only security.

"So what's the plan? You're going upstairs and I'm playing lookout?" I checked the street. It was dead—too hot for foot traffic and, besides, most people were at work. I should be at work.

"Plan?"

"Yeah. Hurry though, it's brutal out here."

"Relax. There's no plan. We're just going to see if she's home."

"Both of us?"

"Sure."

"This is detective work? It's pretty uninspired."

Dan ignored me and ran a finger down the short list of names. He pressed a button and we waited. "I promise this will only take ten minutes. Tops."

"Sure. Did you just buzz Kendal?"

He gave me an odd look. "Yes. Of course."

"Aren't you worried about blowing your cover or something?"

I was pretty sure he rolled his eyes, but it was difficult to tell through those opaque lenses. "I think I know what I'm doing. Will you relax? Ce, sometimes it's this easy."

I sweated as the minutes ticked by and no one answered the buzzer. A delivery truck blasted down the narrow street, leaving a choking trail of exhaust. "It doesn't seem easy this time. Should we go or do you have a *plan B*?"

He pressed another button and within seconds the crabby voice of an elderly woman warbled through the tinny intercom. "Hello? Hello? Who's there? Who's this?"

"Mrs. Rousseau? This is Detective Green—"

I coughed.

"—I'm sorry to trouble you, but I'm trying to locate one of your neighbors. In 4D. Ms. Schmidt."

Just like that, the door buzzer sounded and the lock clicked.

I blinked. "That *was* easy."

"Usually is."

"Doesn't she know it's dangerous to let strangers into the building?" My grandmother would have blistered this woman's ears. I followed Dan past a line of dented mailboxes and into the tiny lobby.

"People hear *cop* and they let you in. You did."

Jesus, he was right. When I thought he was a police officer, I'd let him into all sorts of places. *Personal* places.

We rode the rickety elevator to the fourth floor, where an old woman with a toothless Chihuahua greeted us as soon as the door staggered open. In her white polyester slacks and horn-rimmed glasses, I knew she must be the elderly Mrs. Rousseau.

"Detective?" Apparently the tinny sound hadn't come from a loose wire in the intercom. "I'm Bea Rousseau."

She didn't address me at all—her eyes actually passed over me. Clearly I was no detective. I was the sidekick. A fleet-footed young Robin to Dan's manly Batman.

"Thanks for letting us in," Batman said with no hint of censure. I would have told the woman she was an idiot for opening the door to a pair of strangers, but I wasn't the star of this show.

Dan towered over the pint-sized old lady. He was a cop for fifteen years and when he put his mind to it, there was no question he was law enforcement. He had the tough, squinty-eyed *I think you look like someone I've seen on an arrest warrant* pose that inspired caution in others. So, after he shook Mrs. Rousseau's gnarly hand, she opened the door to Kendal's apartment without bothering with any of the usual formalities. Like asking to see Dan's badge.

The woman was a loon.

She said, "Kendal's been gone for a few days. She always tells me when she's away—but not this time. The last officer who came by was rude and he didn't lock up when he left. Make sure you knock on my door when you're done. We run a tight ship here."

I barely covered a snort, but the smile Dan offered her was

reassuring. "We'll only be a minute. I appreciate it. Mrs. Rousseau, has anyone else been by? Anyone you might have seen? Her boyfriend maybe?"

Mrs. Rousseau's dog growled and sniffed my arm. She drew him away, giving me an offended look. "Charlie, be nice."

I stepped carefully out of bite range, but I knew we must smell like chicken-flavored dog treats.

"Boyfriend? I don't know about that—I haven't seen or heard anyone. I keep an eye on this floor and I call the super when there's trouble. It's been quiet."

Kendal's neighbor toddled back to watch *The Price is Right* and I harped, "Isn't this illegal?"

"Not really. We were let in by a kindly neighbor with a key. We're not building a case. We're not collecting evidence. We're just checking on someone whose welfare we're concerned about."

"Please. I totally don't believe you."

"C'mon. Hop to, let's make this quick."

"See? Your sense of urgency implies that we're breaking the law."

Dan snapped the door shut. "This will only take a minute."

"Wow. Okay. Don't get so testy."

"Holy shit." Dan blinked at Kendal's apartment. The studio was the expected size of a shoebox, though Kendal did have a painted brick fireplace and a two-window view of the street—which must cost extra. One corner held the kitchenette and next to that a tiny bathroom abutted the wall.

What Dan was having a *holy shit* over was the interior. The place was astonishingly different from any apartment in New York I'd ever seen. I swear we'd just stepped inside a Moroccan whorehouse. Floor to ceiling, the place was draped with sumptuously rich textiles. Both windows were festooned with swaths of fine apricot and burgundy silk, all of it fringed with beads in garnet, amethyst and amber. It was like a sultan's den, down to the flea-market rugs—fake Persian, worn and a little musty—and a volume of hastily thrown pillows in wild paisleys and crushed velvets. A swayback table was buried under stacks of coffee-table books and a two-foot fat-assed Buddha squatted on the television. Beside me, a bamboo birdcage was filled with carefully rolled towels and uber organized Miso Pretty bathing products. "This is kind of cool. Is she a pothead?"

"Not that I know of. No misdemeanors—no record. Not even a traffic violation—or a fender bender."

"For the record, this morning was an accident."

"Mmhm. She graduated from NYU a year ago."

"She's a kid."

"Yes. Nearly your age." He stood near the phone, flipping through a notepad on the counter, like he was preparing to make a call. "She was a theater major. Maybe that explains the decor."

"Maybe. It certainly explains why she's a personal assistant." My degree in Art History from Manhattanville had landed me the same sort of illustrious employment—gallery assistant turned caterer.

I wandered the tiny space. Behind a stamped tin screen, a tumble of wild pillows in shiny harem-girl red covered the unmade bed. I couldn't resist running a finger across the silk bedding. Incense and something else...maybe it *was* pot...tickled my nose. It wasn't Les Hommes, that's for sure.

A manga-inspired journal lay open, the spine broken. I had no desire to look into the personal affects of Kendal Schmidt. What I wanted to do was to get the freak out of her apartment, get a sandwich and then go to lunch.

Dan was rattling through the trash can.

"What *are* you doing?"

"Investigating. It's what I do."

"Just wash your hands when you're through." In the center of Kendal's bed lay a well-worn orange tiger cuddled beside a nubby big-bellied panda. "How do you know what you're looking for?"

"Experience."

I made a scoffing noise. "She's got a couple of stuffed animals, a comic book and a fortune in silk charmeuse." The sheets were sinfully expensive and sewn by a skilled hand. What kind of personal assistant can afford to sleep in silk?

I joined Dan in the kitchen. Not *in*, exactly, sort of beside the tiny kitchen. Either Kendal was an anorexic or she was gone because the shelves were empty except for a few dishes. Maybe she had mice and kept everything in the fridge.

Her dorm refrigerator was on top of the counter, decked in snarky, retro-styled Blue-Q magnets. Dan dug a notebook from the kitchen drawer and flipped through it. Mr. Nosy said, "You know what's odd?"

"You mean other than the fact that she lives in a sultan's tent and you're fondling her knickknacks? No. What's odd?"

"No photos. She's got a boyfriend. She has family. She worked for a TV star. I never met a chick who didn't have pictures all over her walls." He nodded toward the refrigerator. "Or stuck to the fridge. Or on the mantle." Her mantle housed a collection of bamboo cricket cages and a row of thirsty African violets. "Where are Kendal and all her friends?"

"Probably buried under that obscenely expensive bedding." But he was right. The apartment felt very personal—and yet faceless. I had a picture on Nan's fridge of myself and my cousin Joey at our cousin Tina's wedding. We were drunk as lords and twice as handsome.

Dan recently stuck a new photo on his Viking fridge—me on his bike.

He disappeared into the bathroom, rattling drawers as he sifted through Kendal's underwear or whatever. This felt so extremely wrong. Like thieves, we were violating her privacy—I had to remember that was Dan's job and he was convinced the girl was missing. We were doing the right thing looking for her.

Right?

I drew a swatch of fabric away from the window and peered outside. The apartment had a perfect view all the way to Christopher Street, and in the other direction fire escapes held potted plants and flowerpots bursting with colorful blossoms. I'd love a place like this, my own space where I could have privacy and autonomy. I'd be close to work. I'd save big bucks in subway fare. I'd be out of the sphere of influence of my family. I could have sex in my own bed.

But I'd be farther from Staten Island.

Dan materialized from the bathroom, and he was equally lost in thought. He viewed Kendal's tiny apartment from a vantage point that was beyond my experience. What did he see that I did not? The apartment was unusual, but nothing appeared amiss to my amateur eye.

He looked through the windows to the empty fire escape, and my stomach gurgled. Dan dropped the curtain and smiled. "Hungry?"

"Little bit. If Kendal is really gone, she'd have cleaned the refrigerator." I went to check. "Yup. There's nothing in her fridge except condiments and diet soda. So..."

"So you deduce that she planned to go. There's no sign of a

struggle, there's no note, no word with the neighbor, no hastily thrown clothing or mess that would lead anyone to think she left in a hurry. It doesn't mean much—she works and maybe she hates to cook—but my gut says she's gone."

I closed the fridge door and a magnet popped off. It slid in the space between the counter and the wall. "Shit."

"I usually avoid breaking anything when I'm investigating."

"Har har. You should have thought of that before you broke in." I wriggled the magnet free, sliding it with a wiggly finger from the wall. *Zippo's Costume Emporium.* A big top hat with Marquee lettering—it sort of reminded me of Shep's invitation. "How did Gun find this chick anyway?"

"Through Estelle. She makes a lot of their decisions. She's the one who put Gun at Shep's for the week. Did you know Shep's assistant, that little twit Stephen, is from Estelle?"

"I'm sure Kendal was more effective." I handed the magnet to Dan. "I think Kendal's a seamstress. Look at this place. I bet she stitched every seam here."

Dan nodded, but the phone rang before he could speak. Damn thing scared the shit out of me. I clutched my chest with a wince. "Jesus."

"Quit being so jumpy." He picked up the phone. Horrified, I expected him to answer, but he just checked the number. "Caller I.D. *Relax.*" He pulled a pad out of his back pocket to write the number down. He used her pen.

"We are getting out of here right now. Peeping and lurking are not in my skill set."

"No kidding. Next time you can wait in the car." Dan's eyes swept me from head to toe and for the first time all day, he got that look. His eyes smoldered and his gaze landed on my mouth. He casually glanced at the bed. "You know what you need to relax? Remember last time—"

"And no hanky-panky either. Jesus." My heart smacked my ribs—which hurt more than I expected. "Let's go. We can have a quickie someplace else. Just not in the car."

"Fine." Dan tapped at the buttons on Kendal's phone and wrote a few things on his pad. "Go get Mrs. Rousseau. I'll be right behind you."

I couldn't leave fast enough.

# Chapter Five: Quickie

Pretty soon we were back on board the elevator of dubious safety. I stabbed the button, the rickety door wobbled shut, and we lurched into motion with a disconcerting crunch. Dan stood innocently beside me, lost once again to his own thoughts. He hogged most of the air in the narrow space, nothing new, and his head nearly brushed the ceiling—it was an old elevator. His jeans hugged his ass. He blinked and thought and chewed his bottom lip, head cocked slightly. He watched the lighted number flicker from 4 to 3. The manly scent of him—minus the chicken because at this point I was blissfully immune to that odor—and his very blandness triggered something in me.

Suspicion.

He had chased me away on purpose. He'd intentionally tricked me into exiting the apartment ahead of him. He'd taken advantage of my discomfort and sent me packing with a single look at that bed.

That *manipulator.*

My eyes narrowed. Goddamn him. I wasn't interested in why he'd sent me away—he'd done me a kindness in a way because when he was arrested, I wouldn't have to lie for him under oath—but it still pissed me off that I'd been so easily handled. He had my number—all the damn time. One of these days, I was going to have his.

I stared at his strong profile. The bold chin. The T-shirt clinging to his pecs. The heavy crotch cupped by his fly. I stared at Dan's bulging package, and my anger morphed into something else. Something earthier. Something that would drive him nuts.

It was time to turn the tables on former NY Detective Dan Albright.

I smacked the *stop* button somewhere between 3 and 2 and let Dan stumble as the elevator brake snagged. That gave me a little thrill of pleasure. He caught himself with a hand to the door, and the look he sent me was cautious. "Problem?"

"I just need a minute." No alarm rang, and looking around, I didn't see a security camera, not that it mattered to us. I stuffed my hand into my pocket and chose my words with care. "You're a dick."

His mouth fell open. "Hey, Romano. That's not nice."

"And you are nice?" I advanced on him. "You know what? Because of you, I was late to work—"

"Not by that much."

"I smashed three cars—"

"Now, Caesar, you can't put that one on me."

"—been lied to—"

"Nope. Not by me."

"By omission. And now I've come dangerously close to committing a felony—"

He snorted.

"You knew she wasn't going to be there—you'd never risk exposing yourself so...so blithely. You're supposed to stay under the radar."

"You read too much."

"—and now I smell like a dumpster—"

"It's not that bad. I can't even smell you anymore."

"You dick. You did something in that apartment. Took something. Planted something. Found something." I poked his chest with a fingertip.

"I just—"

"Don't you dare tell me."

Dan wisely snapped his mouth shut.

"I don't want to know what you did. You know what I think? I think you owe me. I've been accommodating all day and I think it's your turn to accommodate me."

I peeled my shirt over my head and tossed it into the corner of the elevator. I forgot my sore ribs as his dirty, surprised grin made my blood boil. A hot river of lust flooded straight to my groin—exactly where I wanted it. My dick was hard before my shirt hit the ground.

"Oh, baby, I do owe you. I'll give you anything you like." His submission was all talk because he stalked me now, corralling me against the elevator wall.

I smiled deviously as his eyes searched my face. "You bet you will."

"Jesus I can't decide what to do first. You drive me nuts."

"Just make it quick and mind my lip."

His smile hitched to the left. "Your wish is my command..."

Dan's touch hovered just a hairsbreadth from my skin. His fingertips moved from my chin, down across my chest, nearly touching me, but not quite. My nipples hardened and I sucked in a laugh. "I wish you'd touch me, then."

"You'll forgive me the entire day if I do? You want me to

suck you? Right here? Maybe Mrs. Rousseau needs to walk her dog. Maybe she'll call the super because the elevator's stuck."

"Maybe she will." My voice was so low he had to lean close to hear. His shirt brushed my skin. I dug a finger into Dan's belt and hauled him against me. "You better hurry it up then, Albright."

He feathered his lips on mine. "Tell me what you want, Ce."

I wouldn't say it...not out loud, so I settled for, "I want you to put your mouth on me."

He was on his knees in a split second. My belt clacked in the stuffy elevator, and I thought my knees might buckle my head was so light. He peeled my pants down my thighs and exposed me. Wet, hot, heated lips swallowed the swollen tip of my erection, and I relaxed and let the wall support me. The only noise in the space was the soft sucking of Dan's perfect mouth as he pulled the smooth fat length of my cock into his throat—and the ringing in my ears as I hyperventilated myself into an easy orgasm.

# Chapter Six: Ridin' that Train

I spent the afternoon inside Posh Nosh paying bills and prepping for Friday's grand fiasco à la McNamara. Lunch, a/c and mind-blowing elevator sex had put me in a great mood. Dan had forced me to take four Motrin for the alarming purple bruise spreading across my rib cage. Poppy was still at the doctor's seeing to her womanly area. She texted me periodically, offering her typical TMI via my cell.

*I've gained seven pounds, you lying fucker.*

*Ultrasound chick had garlic for lunch. Tic Tac? Anyone? OMG.*

*Do you think I'm emotional?*

*Leave the cake alone. I know you.*

*Do you miss me?*

*I feel like they should pay me and not the other way around. They put a condom on that ultrasound wand and then they stuck it right up my—*

Snap! That was enough of Poppy for one afternoon. I set my phone to vibrate and went to dig through our storage. Cutlery, glassware, crockery, paper goods, linens, booze—anything remotely Oscar-themed I boxed and loaded into the van to take uptown. The last thing I was personally responsible for at this point was waitstaff, and, as Poppy stated no less than five times, a tuxedo for the weekend—I wasn't wearing Joey's. I refused to attend the Soapies looking like a flashback to the '70s.

It felt later than six when I locked the door, but on the street the light of day nearly blinded me. The air was in a semi-solid state, stifling with humidity and smog and the sweat of a million weary commuters. It was like any other summer evening in the Village. I locked Posh Nosh and headed to the subway.

Locals swarmed the streets, the majority of them licking ice cream cones or runny popsicles. The hotdog cart was conveniently parked near the bus stop—that was a clever combination of odors—and both lines moved slowly. The hotdog man wore a sorry-looking hotdog on his head. Close to the cart, bums aired their blackened feet on the front stoop of an apartment building. Dogs and small children were out for their evening walk, each complaining in their own whimpering way.

To a being, everyone appeared limp and moist.

I'd been spoiled by air-conditioning all afternoon, so I hit the entrance to the subway at a trot. I needed to get to Rocco's before my father went home for the night.

I took the filthy stairs, fingers far from the railing—that thing was a glorified Petri dish just waiting to infect me with the plague—and raced down to the turnstile. As I did, I swear to God, someone watched me. A combination of hair standing to attention on my forearms, and a niggling feeling that I'd forgotten something, had me doing the most natural and telling thing in the world. I looked over my shoulder. No one stood out in the sea of rush-hour humanity. I didn't recognize any faces, and nobody seemed to notice me. I was just another fit, firm Italian. Just another kid from Brooklyn headed home.

I moved with the fleeing multitude, rustling through my bag

for my transit pass, which, now that I was flipping through my satchel, was nowhere to be found. Goddamn it. I dug deeper. I'm fairly organized. I like things in order—I enjoy lists and labeled plastic bins and sharpies that mark with permanence. I may procrastinate, but I do so neatly.

My card was absent from my bag, and that sucker was worth ninety dollars. At least new it was. Now it had about seventy bucks remaining. I was broke enough that buying a new one would pinch my already constrained budget.

At the bottom of the stairs, away from the pedestrian flow, I checked every compartment, pocket, slot and fold. My bag was a disaster. I hadn't straightened it since the earlier spill that nuisance photojournalist caused with his overcompensating telephoto lens—and as much as I didn't like it, I'd have to wait until I was home to set my bag to rights.

I sifted through my belongings. I still had my full arsenal of condoms—but no transit pass. Maybe in my rush to Shep's, I put it in my wallet.

Relief was fleeting, because inside my wallet—check—my NYC Transit Authority thirty-day pass. I felt ridiculously as if I'd found seventy dollars, and then I realized my driver's license wasn't behind its little plastic window.

I emptied my pockets. My workbag. Carefully searching my wallet again. I publicly groped myself in search of my license, and all it yielded was four dollars and another ribbed condom. Electric blue. This wasn't simple optimism—my love life had taken a terrific turn for the better.

I'd seen my I.D. this morning, handing it through the window to that thick-fingered psycho at Cappy's Luxury Auto Sales and then...I guess that tattooed bastard hadn't returned it.

I crammed everything into my bag. The very last thing I

wanted to do in this lifetime was revisit the scene of the accident. *Accidents.* It was six oh eight. It would have to wait for tomorrow.

The back of my neck itched as I fed my transit pass into the turnstile and hurried through the filthy tunnel down to the platform. After the long day, with no sexcapade to look forward to tonight, I was going home to my lonely bed.

Stuffy, filthy and fetid—the New York City subway in the summer wasn't for the weak or the uninitiated. It wasn't great for the unemployed either because a grown man in a grimy lipstick costume, sandwiched between two tired blondes in pink Max Factor T-shirts, careened along the platform. He swayed on toothpick legs encased in hot pink tights, shaking hands flaccidly with a few cringing commuters. Mr. Lipstick knocked into a suited businessman, and the typical jostling and foul language ensued. "Watch where you're going, dipstick."

I moved farther along the platform. Frayed tempers were par for the course, even this early in the season, and it was best to keep one's distance. Besides, I didn't want to come face-to-face with that poor bastard. He could be any one of us down on our luck. He'd taken a job so low on the totem pole, who could dare look him in the eye? If not for Poppy, that could have been me.

I was happy to lose sight of the lipstick as the screech of the subway filled the tunnel. The crowd swelled and we surged forward.

Something smacked the small of my back, and I stumbled toward the edge of the platform. Unable to turn in the clog of commuters, I leaned backward as smudged windows flickered past my nose. My ride home came to a noisy halt an inch from my chest.

My heart slammed against my sore ribs. *God.* I'd nearly

fallen over the edge of the platform—right onto the tracks. I'd have gone right under the damn train. Crushed and electrocuted by the F train. I could have headlined tomorrow's paper.

I caught my breath and the doors opened. Testy New Yorkers exited and entered the subway en masse. Protocol dictated that those alighting had the right of way, but that was weak, so seconds after my brush with death, I crammed myself halfway through the door. This time I took a hit directly in the center of my purpling bruise. A bag or a fist or some small child's head—whatever it was, it sent a bolt of excruciating pain across my solar plexus. White light danced behind my eyes and nausea tightened my gut.

*Please don't let me puke.*

I stumbled, catching myself on the open doorway. My knee connected with the platform and I clung to the metal frame of the subway door by my fingertips. I'd be trampled if I hit the ground. Of course, I'd die a worse death if my bare skin came in contact with the bacteria-coated surface of the subway platform. People *spat* on that ground. Hell, they pissed on it.

I tried to find my attacker, but I was knee level to the crowd. People literally climbed over me, the heartless bastards. My side burned. My stomach rolled.

"You okay?" a man thought to ask. He gave me a hand, which I took gratefully.

I licked my upper lip and the subway chimed its warning. Before the doors shut on me, I groped past the pain and let the kind man yank me into the car.

"That was close."

"Thank you."

"Yeah, be careful. You could get crushed."

I slung my bag to the front in a lame, belated effort to protect my injury and squirmed through the sardine-packed car, finding purchase as another bell rang and the door slammed shut.

The train was full of bored commuters. Most faces were buried in newspapers or books. Nobody stood out. Everyone looked irritated and ready to get home. Overheated. Overworked. They appeared as they always did.

And that's precisely when I knew someone *was* following me. Dan had warned me that it's never the obvious person, the one in the dark glasses and the false mustache you had to watch for. It's the one you can't make, even when you know he's right there.

I dug in my bag for my iPod and lost myself to Muse thinking about Dan Albright and the phone conversation we would have later this evening.

Outside my window, the pointy peaked head of the lipstick man bobbled above the thinning crowd.

We lurched and the car entered the blackened tunnel.

Half hour later, I was safely in my father's restaurant, squinting in the scarlet glare. My father equated *class* with the sort of depth of color one usually associated with *crass*. Brothels, any pick of Chinese restaurants in the city—or the color of Kendal Schmidt's apartment. Velvet-and-Mylar-flocked wallpaper, florid carpeting, crimson chandeliers and glossy vinyl booths—dining at Rocco's lent one a rather sanguine complexion.

My ironically blond brother Paulie hovered behind the bar chatting with his wife Donna, the dental hygienist from Long Island. She had unnaturally white teeth and boasted a teased Long Island claw that was ten years out of fashion. I like

Donna—God bless her, she puts up with Paulie—but she's got it tough. My parents were tapping their toes, checking their calendars and measuring Donna's unchanging waistline with their looks. They wanted grandchildren and because they weren't ever going to get them from this quarter, Paulie and his wife were charged with securing our old man's immortality. Sooner rather than later.

I waved an absent hello to my brother and headed to the booth where my petite mother was tucked in her usual spot with her low-calorie supper: pasta fagioli, a dry house salad and an even drier vodka martini.

She smiled as I approached. My mom's a funny little thing. She's not Italian, but she puts up a good front. My father's family is fierce, loyal and operating mostly aboveboard. There were things it was better not knowing, and Ellie Cooper Romano was nobody's fool. She sipped her drink and scooted over. "Caesar. Give me a kiss and ask your brother to bring you a bowl of soup."

I pecked her powdered cheek and sat down. She slid her salad my way and I dug in, stopping first to pour oil and red wine vinegar liberally over the top. "You're done with this right?"

She nodded. "So. What's new? Why are you here on Wednesday?"

"Poppy. She roped me into something unsavory and I need help."

"Unsavory?" She gave me her mom look, and those carefully plucked brows scrunched together. "You? That's not like either of you. It's not illegal, is it?"

"No, Mom. It's just unappetizing."

"Immoral?"

"No. *Mom.* It's a nuisance."

"It must be for you to come for help." She leaned back into the bench and sipped her martini. Her shellacked helmet of hair was perfectly ordered.

"I know. I'm in a bind. I need some staff for Friday night, and I'm flat out of ideas. I figured maybe Pop could steer me in the right direction."

As if I'd invoked him, my father pushed through the swinging kitchen doors. He snuck behind the counter and turned Tony Bennett up a notch, and then he came over, untying his apron as he did so.

"Hey," my father said as he slipped into the booth. "What's wrong? You hungry?"

I get my medium height from the Cooper side of the family—and my propensity toward prissiness. Everything else, I get from my father. Wild hand gesturing, snap decisions, my swarthy good looks and speedy metabolism—all credited to Rocco Romano. The queer thing was anyone's guess. They all swear I'm the first.

Pop snapped his fingers at my brother. "Paulie—get your brother a drink."

I cringed and started to get up. "I wish you wouldn't do that. I can get something myself."

"Sit." Pop flagged my brother over while asking me, "What's a matter? That Dan giving you trouble?"

"Why do you always ask that? Everything's fine. I came by because I need to find some waiters for Friday night. I have this upcoming series of unfortunate events...and I need discreet, trustworthy people who aren't impressed by celebrity."

"Discreet? In Brooklyn? Ha. Good luck." My father went to sneak a sip of my mother's drink, and she poked the back of his hand with her fork. "Hey."

"Mind your hands, Roc."

He winked and my mother rolled her eyes.

I stayed the course. "I know, but I have no option. This is for a celebrity event. I spent the afternoon on the phone—nada. I can't hire people I don't know."

My father glanced around the restaurant and muttered, "Friday night, you say? That's a busy night."

"I'm not planning to mooch—although maybe someone who's not on the schedule could moonlight for Posh Nosh? It's for Poppy." He loved Poppy. Everyone in my family loved Poppy, especially Joey.

"Maybe." He didn't sound encouraging. "I just don't have anyone to spare—private party Friday night. I would if I could."

Paulie arrived with two glasses of Chianti, one he handed to me, and the other he sipped. "Hey. It's not Saturday. What are you doing here?"

My dad pointed two fingers at me. "Caesar needs help with a problem."

"Yeah no kidding. You knock someone up?"

I made my *ha ha very funny* face at him.

My mother said testily, "Did *you*? You should be working on that and not giving your brother a hard time."

"You want I should do that right now?" Paulie's grin was unapologetic. "I told you, Ma, I'm working on it."

Pop still glared at me like I was poaching on his staff. I hastened to assure him, "I only need two waiters, that's it. One evening."

"Two? I can maybe find you one."

"Uh. Plus I need a bartender."

"That's three. Not one. You're the college boy—didn't they

teach you math at Manhattanville?" The table jerked and wine sloshed in their glasses as my mother kicked him. "What? Why'd you kick me?"

"You should ask that boyfriend of yours," Paulie cut in. "I bet he could mix a drink or two. How hard is it to make a Cosmo? He seems capable."

"Dan? Hah."

"What? He'd do it. Just ask him."

"Dan? That's...he...that's..."

"He thinks you hung the moon. He'd do it."

"I wouldn't go that far, but..." I leaned against the vibrant upholstery and considered my brother. Inconceivable. Paulie was on to something. Dan would be in the apartment anyway, and he'd want to blend and lurk. Peep and Tom. Shift his eyes. Like he always did.

Maybe he was going to stand at the door like a hulking bouncer and check his list against I.D.s for gatecrashers? I couldn't picture it. He'd hire people for that kind of grunt work. I remembered all the times Dan the chameleon had disappeared in plain sight, flying under the radar—he was damned good at it for such a big guy, and for this party? He'd want to be in the thick of things with no one the wiser.

Paulie drank his Chianti and looked smugly back at me.

"Holy smokes," I said to him, "that's actually a great idea."

"Hey, don't look so surprised." He tapped my wineglass with his. "*Salud.* I still got it."

"You oughta use it on Donna." I winked.

Paulie sauntered back to the bar, and my mother smiled. "He's a good boy. I want grandchildren, and he's dragging his feet."

"I don't think it's his feet he's dragging."

She pursed her lips and her keen eyes looked shrewd. "How bad you need the help?"

"Bad. I'm out of options because I can't hire anyone I don't know." Which left off enticing any staff away from the competition.

"Okay. I know who'll do it." She was brisk and pleased. "They're trustworthy—as long as you tell them not to take anything—they won't tattle, and they're both free agents on Friday nights. They don't give a fig about movie stars, either."

"Really? That sounds perfect. Who did you have in mind?"

"Ellie." Pop looked pained. "*Mia famiglia*? You're not thinking—"

"Tino and Vito. You won't have to pay them. And they'll maybe give Dan some guidance. Did he introduce you to his parents yet?"

Tino and Vito? She was insane. "How much have you had to drink?"

She stared expectantly at me. What else had she asked? Oh God. Dan's parents.

I swallowed. This had become a bone of contention. Not between Dan and me because he didn't seem to mind that I kept postponing week after week—possibly he hadn't noticed. This was an issue between my mother and me. "It's only been a month and a half. It's not...time for that. I'm not marrying the guy, for God's sake." My parents exchanged a look that wasn't at all discreet, and I knocked back my wine in two swallows. Marriage. Holy ever lovin' Christ. It wasn't even legal. Yet. "I was supposed to go to Westchester on Saturday, but something came up."

"Something always comes up. You want me to speak with him?" My tiny mother looked bland, but let me assure you she was concocting a plan to drag me down the aisle.

I didn't look good in white, and something told me Dan wasn't ready for Italian in-laws. It had only been *six weeks.*

My collar felt unusually tight. "No. No. No. Something came up with me, not with him. I gotta go. But, thanks. That's a great idea about Vito and Tino. I'll call them tonight."

I'd have the most memorable catering staff those gilded-lily actors had ever seen. The entire *Days* cast would get a crash Uta Hagen workshop in method characterization. No one did Brooklyn Italian like the Romanos—well no one did and lived to tell about it.

The vision of Tino and Vito dressed in aprons, foisting tandoori chicken skewers on D-list actors—well? I had to admit, it gave me a touch of indigestion.

Rocco's is a fair distance from my nana's house. Being a hale and hearty twenty-eight-year-old who'd had a tad too many lemon squares and M&M's today, I opted to walk home. The Motrin had worn off, but I could handle this. I said bye to my folks, gave Donna a quick nod and left. I had another reason to call Dan tonight. How the hell would I ask him to serve drinks to soap opera divas?

Outside, the heat of the day had risen to form a bright orange pall of smog that hung directly above Brooklyn. Rings of streetlight dotted the concrete, and ahead, folks dined al fresco at Pop's competition—Palmeri's. An odorous Staten Island breeze cooled the neighborhood.

My reflection was still visible in the plate-glass window, only five feet from Rocco's vermillion front door, when the unsettling feeling of being watched returned. What could I do but keep walking? I wasn't going to scurry back to my family, so I settled my bag over my shoulder and hit the curb by the alley. As I did, a pair of scarred hands reached from the shadows and jerked me by the shirt collar into the darkness. "Wha—?"

Silencing me with a broad palm to my big mouth, Dan dragged me under the fire escape like some caveman's unwilling bride. I swung an elbow into his gut. "MRrfhphg!"

"*Oof.* Knock it off." His mouth brushed my ear. "Someone's following you."

*Again?* We'd been here before, with Dan surprising the piss out of me and then transferring the blame. The scent of him, that tangy blend of mint, nicotine and spice, should have eased me—or aroused me. Instead it infuriated me. I peeled his hand from my face. "Ouch. Yes. You're following me. Déjà vu."

"Right. That's what you said last time and six people showed up."

"You have to stop doing this."

"You said that too. I will stop doing this—which is called saving your ass from hassle by the way—when you start paying attention. Caesar, you're oblivious." He had the gall to scold me as he led me farther into shadows. We ducked into a hidden doorway beneath the rusted fire escape. He nodded toward the street. "There's a guy watching Rocco's."

"I'm not oblivious. I knew someone was tailing me. You would only know that if you were watching Rocco's as well."

"I'm following a lead. I told your stalker to take a hike, but I'm sure he circled the block. You know him."

"Know him?" Try as I might, I couldn't see anyone on the sidewalk. All looked quiet on that front. "Are you sure?"

Dan tucked me into his much larger body, arms wrapped loosely around my waist. He stuck his thumbs in my back pockets and copped a quick feel. I gripped his shirtfront, undecided whether I was hanging on to get a feel myself or getting a firm grip to shove him into the metal ladder for scaring me.

We were angled toward the street. Behind us, the back door to my pop's restaurant was propped open and yellow light splashed the broken pavement. The dishwasher's rapid Spanish drifted on the night air.

I narrowed my eyes at Dan. "Are you making this up? You're not doing this to get a quick grope in a quasi-public place, are you? Wasn't the elevator enough?"

"Not this time."

"So the elevator wasn't enough?"

Dan was hot, sweaty and sticky, and while I was concerned about the danger he believed was close at hand, I felt safe here. My father's restaurant was on the one side, Dan was on the other. I was in Brooklyn. What could happen?

He was terribly distracting. I flattened my palms on his chest and felt the rhythm of his heart. Strong and steady. His hips snuggled mine. As expected, his dick was making its presence known. A little thrill shot through my jockeys and I perked up too.

We were certainly a pair.

True to form, Dan whispered, "Although, since we're here..."

He moved against me and I stopped him with a smile. "Sometimes I wonder if you're insane."

"You definitely make me crazy."

"Why are you in Brooklyn? I thought you were working—having your big gay sleepover with Gun and Shep."

Speaking those words aloud made the situation seem much tawdrier. I pictured the three of them snapping welts on each other's bare bottoms with wet towels as they streaked through Shep's over-decorated bachelor pad. The word ménage flittered briefly through my mind and I frowned.

"I left those two practicing their acceptance speeches. I hired someone to watch the hall. I can't find Schmidt and babysit the German at the same time."

"Who's there? Someone from the force?"

"I have a few people lined up. Don't get excited—"

That gave me pause and I moved back. "Do you have any idea how much it irritates me when people say that? I don't get excited."

"John is working for me. You met him earlier today."

I sifted through the day and the only person I could think of was—

"You're joking."

He glared at the mouth of the alley. "Shhh. Keep your voice down."

"My voice is down. I'm enunciating with emphasis."

"Sure."

"That's who you have watching the hall? The blond from the car dealership?"

Dan's dark eyes gleamed. In the shadows, he looked dangerous. "You're not jealous are you?"

"*Pffft*. Dream on."

His hands caressed me—feeling carefully, almost gingerly, as if he realized for the first time that he could hurt me. Fingertips trailed my ribs and I held my breath. His palm slid down my spine and my toes curled. His voice went low. "You don't need to be jealous."

"Don't I?" It slipped out before I could stop it.

"No."

Shit. I looked away, keeping my eyes peeled for danger—looking anywhere but at Dan. He was the real danger here. I should keep my eye on him, but he saw too much.

A car drove by. Otherwise it was still, but not quiet.

Dan leaned heavily into me until my back met the wall. I stumbled on something—I didn't want to know what filthy thing was on the ground—and he grabbed me to keep me upright. I hissed in pain, and he whispered, "Sorry." Lips caressed my neck. "I won't lie. I like it. Just a little. You're feisty when you're jealous."

"I'm going to feisty you in the nuts in a second."

"That sounds kinda kinky." He nibbled my lower lip, and our late day whiskers scraped together. I bent enough to kiss him back, my tongue darting to taste his, and he smiled against my lips. "You had wine. You're sweet."

"You're on crack. I am anything but sweet."

"You were pretty sweet this afternoon." Dan's dick thickened by the second. Mine too. I stole another taste—mint. He'd been chewing that gum he liked. The guy was fucking irresistible. His hand smoothed along my back and he asked, "How are your ribs?"

"I'm fine."

"No. You're favoring your left side more than you were at lunch. You keep hissing and jerking when I touch you. You want me to come back and tape that for you?" He licked my lip.

"Maybe. Tell me why you hired the guy from the dealership to watch the hall."

He gave up on his seduction with a sigh. "He used to...work for me. He can handle this. We've got it covered...and I told you, I'm following a lead."

"Me? You're following me. *Again.* How is it I'm a suspect a second time?"

"You're not a suspect, but it's uncanny how you always

wind up in the thick of things."

Movement on the street and we both zipped our traps. Dan's hand froze on my backside, his fingers deeply tucked in the ass seam of my denim.

It wasn't that much of a shocker when Jorge Carrera skulked past the mouth of the alley. I recognized him by the camera drooping obscenely from his waist and that sickly phony tail hanging lank from the back of his head. He took a cautious step in our direction, but a noise from the other side of the street sent him scurrying onward. "That's the photographer from earlier."

I couldn't tell what Dan was thinking. "I can see that. Why is he following you?"

"Maybe he's looking for a good time."

Dan gave me a look.

"What? It's possible."

"No, he's after something."

"He offered to pay me for an exclusive interview. He wants a new angle on the life and times of the closeted Mr. Potter."

"This isn't about Shep. That photographer is after you—he wants something else. If you see Carrera again, tell him you'll press charges."

"That seems extreme. Can I do that?"

"If he persists—yes. If it gets worse, let me know, and I'll chat with him personally."

"Hey, way to emasculate me. I can handle this. I knew someone was following me earlier. It must have been Jorge."

Dan pulled back enough to frown at me. "You were serious? When."

"On the ride from work. He could have watched me all day. Although, I should have seen him."

"Gun's car. It's possible whoever was following him, made you at the dealership. I mean, it was hard not to."

I didn't find him funny in the least. "He has no reason to watch me. What do I matter? Did I piss someone off?"

Dan blinked innocently. "It happens."

"Thanks a lot."

"I have a bad feeling. I can't shake it. I'm going with my gut. Something feels off—since earlier."

"Remember that I'm not involved in this. I'm just paying for my bad luck with men."

"Hey."

I patted him. "My previous bad luck with men."

"You should come back with me tonight. We can have our own slumber party."

"Tempting as that sounds—and it does—I'm going home tonight and getting some sleep." And do some laundry. I kept the boring domestic details to myself.

"Was I insensitive?"

"Maybe. Sleeping under Shep's roof isn't cool with me. And if Jean Luc's staying at the apartment too, I don't think there are walls thick enough in New York State to protect us from hearing the kind of things I'd rather not hear."

I'd found a lot of mysterious sex equipment in the bathroom the one time I'd snooped at Shep's. Jean and Shep had a pretty kinky thing going on. Not that there was anything wrong with kinky—I had my own proclivities. I was simply more conservative and discreet. Discounting the times Dan and I had sex nearly in public. "I'm sure they're loud."

"So are you."

"I am not loud."

“You want to rethink that? I have teeth marks on my hand from earlier.”

“You exaggerate.”

“We could do that again right here.” He rocked into my cock and that was all it took. I went stiff with lust. His hot breath tickled my ear. “Next time I could gag you. That’s something we haven’t tried. I want to. Do you want me to? I could tie you to my bed—stuff something in your mouth. What would turn you on? Underwear?”

My skin prickled with shame and longing. “You’re depraved.”

“So are you, baby. You’ll like it. I promise. Maybe tomorrow night, we could take this back to my place—I can practice tying knots.”

“Boy Scout.”

“Hey. I’m not the one walking around the city with a bag full of condoms.” He slid my satchel from my shoulder and, smiling, his hand found my bulging crotch. “I promise not to hurt your ribs.” He dragged a hand along the ridge of my cock, and I rolled into his palm. I licked the salty line from his jaw to his shoulder.

My teeth came together in a tiny nip.

“Oh. Yeah. Bite me, Ce. I wanted you all day. Since I last had you. Why do I want you all the fucking time? I can’t get enough of you.”

“Well here I am.”

“Here you are.” He stroked my mouth with the rough pads of two fingertips. He traced the soft line on my lips until I sucked them in. Dan hissed.

I licked under his knuckles, and Dan’s eyelids fluttered shut.

A door slammed and I spat his fingers out. "Jesus. Seriously. We can't do this here. My father—"

"No one can see us." His hand never left the front of my jeans—in fact, he was dragging my fly down and stroking insistently. "Why don't I just..."

My cock was hard enough to stretch right through my Hugo Boss underwear into Dan's eagerly waiting fingers. He could wrap his fist around and jerk me off quick. We could do this. Fast. We were practiced at it.

Dan nuzzled my ear. "We're going to fuck right here. You ever do this at the restaurant?"

"Right here? Yeah," I said dreamily, and his hand closed a bit too tight on my dick. "Ow." I opened my eyes to find a strange look on his face. What had I said?

Oh. Oops.

I stuttered, "I...I...uh...not *here* here. But...you know, here...sort of...here." I stopped talking because I couldn't possibly lie to him—but the truth wasn't sexy. I'd had sex in the restaurant years ago—probably the first time I experienced the seedier side of lust—and at the time I didn't realize how much I liked it. Six weeks in Dan's arms had taught me a thing or two about myself and my propensity toward public sex.

I fumbled and Dan gaped at me. "You're fucking kidding me."

"What?"

"You and that dope McNamara? Here?" He went from surprised to amused, and his grin deepened. That arrogant dick scolded me again. "Well, well, well. Mr. Caesar Romano had a blow job in the men's room."

"It's not groundbreaking."

"I bet for you it was. I love that about you." With a neat

hand trick, he unbuttoned my jeans and flicked my belt loose. Hope sprung—my cock with it—and Dan wriggled my jeans until my erection leaped into his skilled hand.

I panted, "We could...do this. No one can see us right?"

"Does it fucking matter anymore?" He finally let loose, his mouth searing mine, his tongue burrowing deep. I ripped at his shirt, yanking it up to feel the puckered bands under my hands. The contrast of smooth and rough—it undid me. Why those angry burns turned me on was further testament of my insane lust for this one man.

We wrestled under the fire escape, groping each other, fighting to get a hold or a hand—something—anything but a grip on self-control. All day I'd waited, well since this morning's elevator adventure—Jesus there was always an adventure to be had with him. He was as addictive as any drug, and I was desperate for Dan to give me a fix. I needed it. Right now.

His rough hand caressed my dick, and the friction I craved was almost there.

"Harder." I squirmed and fought to free him from his clothing. "Come on."

The noise of cars on the street and laughter on the sidewalk—the conversation in Spanish just around the corner, the smell of pasta and spice and yesterday's garbage—my circuits overloaded the second his erection landed in my palm.

Dan wrestled my hand away. "Let me do it." He fisted our cocks together, handling them like he always did—tough love—and he was about to bring me off. "Yeah, that's it, baby. Fuck me."

I bit him hard. Lip. Neck. Down to the slash of his clavicle. I fucked his prick, and he didn't bother to shush either of us—he just kept bossing me around. "Make some noise, you little fucker. You like it? Tell me. Tell me how much you like it."

"I...oh shit...I..." Footsteps on the street...someone was coming. "Someone's coming...someone's coming..."

"Yeah, I'm coming." Dan latched onto my neck, drawing hard enough that I winced—and that was even more exhilarating. His hand jerked. I squeezed—eyes, ass, fists in his hair—and he soaked me with come. Wet hot semen made my glide easier. My knees shook, and Dan pinned me with his own quaking shoulders into the brick wall as orgasm threatened to tear me in half.

"Oh shit...shit..."

His words were dark. "Tell me."

Then the back door opened and a voice rang out, feet hit the steps, lights flashed, people were coming. They were coming. They'd see. They'd see us tucked in the shadows, our pants down, Dan's bare ass clenching as he thrust into me...and...sparks erupted behind my eyelids. *Shit.* My lover's mouth on my neck, his hand slapping my cock and I ruptured—coming... "Coming...I'm coming..."

"Fuck yeah you are."

Release made me weak and thick-headed, but Dan held me up as I sucked muggy city air into my bruised lungs.

Rocco's Spanish-speaking dishwasher strolled the alley, a cigarette glowing in his hand. He didn't look our way, but that didn't mean he was unaware. This was New York. People witnessed back alley sex every day.

Of course, if he said a word to my brother, I'd never live it down.

Dan's hands were slathered, but he was smiling. "We're a mess."

Sated, "No biggie," was all I could manage. He chuckled against me. We did our best to clean each other, tucking shirts and zipping flies—my belt clacked again—and then we slipped from the alley, his hand in mine.

Dan said, "You are the most outrageous person I've ever met."

"Then you don't get out much." But I squeezed his fingers.

"I think Carrera's gone. If he bothers you, set him straight."

"Aye, aye. Will do."

"Sure you don't want to come back to the city with me?"

I nodded. "Yeah. I'll see you in the morning."

Dan climbed into that foul-smelling white Camry, six pine tree air fresheners swinging valiantly from the rearview mirror, and he drove into the orange night.

And I still hadn't told him that Saturday in Westchester was off.

# Chapter Seven: Stewed

Rattling bracelets heralded Nana's entry into the kitchen. "Good morning, sunshine," she said, and made a beeline for the coffeepot. Her face was a makeup-enhanced pink at six a.m., but her hose were still rolled below her knee. The royal purple slippers and housedress suited her blonde hair—currently wrapped like yellow taffy around sausage-thick rollers. A newspaper was tucked under her arm.

"Morning. Did you get the paper? I wondered where it was."

"Now, pumpkin, I need to tell you something." She hustled to refill my mug.

"I can get my own. You don't have to do that."

"Don't be silly." She was in a hurry. There must be an event planned today—library, museum, shopping, tango lessons, a show. It was no different than any other day for my socializing grandmother. May Cooper was not going gently into that good night. Instead, she was going to take a busload of Manhattan-bound thrill-seeking seniors with her—and they were all going to have discount shoes and knock-off handbags from Canal Street.

I poured myself a hearty bowl of Rice Krispies and ladled three teaspoon of sugar over the top. After a reassuring *snap, crackle and pop*, I dug in.

Never one to beat around the bush, Nan slapped the paper next to my placemat. "You need to see this, pumpkin."

I met her concerned look, put down my spoon and retrieved the paper. "Something big happen?"

"You tell me."

I sipped my coffee and scanned the headlines.

*Mr. Potter Ex declares "Vengeance Is Mine"*

Coffee spattered my very first ever newspaper appearance as I choked. For the first time since I'd taken four aspirin and wrapped myself in athletic tape, my ribs twinged painfully. There it was in horrific gray scale—my detestably unattractive driver's license photo. Below it, in 14 fucking point font, read the caption:

*Former Secretary Caesar Anthony Romano*

They listed my age as *twenty-nine*, the misinformed and mathematically challenged imbeciles. My birthday was months away. And, *hello*, I'd been an art gallery *assistant*. My mother was going to have a heart attack.

I scanned the article as my Rice Krispies absorbed milk. "I never said any of this. How did they know I was...oh my God. That asshole, Carrera. How did he get this?"

"Caesar. Language." Upset or not, Nan wasn't permissive when it came to cussing. She poured kitty chow into a ceramic dish, and Bella waddled into the kitchen, eager for breakfast. She twined around my grandmother's sturdy ankles. "Why didn't you mention any of this yesterday?"

"I forgot. Honestly, the day was packed with so many catastrophes by the time I got home...it was late..." And Dan had relaxed me so completely that I came home, took a shower and a Percocet and fell asleep. "The accident slipped my mind."

There were a lot of things best kept from Nana and the entire Romano clan. I might have tape on my ribs, but my lip was fine—no telltale injury there. The entire incident would have been forgotten if not for Carrera and whatever snitch had handed him my license. I only prayed no one in my family clipped this article and stuck it to the refrigerator. And then...a new thought had me squeezing my eyes shut.

"Do Vito and Tino know?" My uncles would think nothing of sizing cement galoshes for Jorge.

"I don't know. It's still early."

Everyone in the five boroughs could see this wretched picture. My stomach tightened—and my twenty-one-year-old visage stared stylishly back at me. "Shit."

Nan smacked my head.

"Shoot. Sorry. I hate this picture."

"It is a hideous picture—and your license is expired, Caesar."

"What? No it's still good."

"Well, maybe nobody will recognize you. I told you to get a new photo years ago. I never understood the mustache."

"I thought I was dashing—like a young Valentino. I was a kid, Nan." How many times would I need to repeat that phrase *now*? I rubbed my hand across my upper lip. I needed to shave—and this photo reminded me that I would shave every single day for the rest of my life. I looked like a bookie.

"You look like a bookie. It's the hair too."

"I hoped to appear older. I was tired of being carded."

"Did it work?"

"Not really. Mostly people tried to get an inside track on the races."

"Why didn't you get a new one?"

"I kept meaning to, but it's valid until my birthday." And spending a day in the motor vehicle department seemed an extreme measure simply to soothe my vanity. So I'd procrastinated and paid the price.

I scanned the article, if you could call that flagrant abuse of the first amendment a news article. Carrera stated that I'd incurred a hundred fifty thousand dollars worth of damage in my "desperate" attempt to attract famed Shep McNamara's notice. The ace reporter surmised I'd followed Gunter Heidelbach's car to Cappy's in hopes of a confrontation with Shep's new lover.

"*Jealous rage*? Why would I be jealous of Heidelbach? I mean he's more appealing than Shep..."

Nan asked mildly, "Really? That's juicy. Did you meet him? Did Dan? What does he think of Gunter?"

"Slow down. I'm just stating a fact. The man is attractive if you go for that sort of thing. Dan thinks about what you'd expect Dan to think. He's not impressed by celebrity—his uncle's a senator, for Pete's sake."

Nana waved that off. "That's entirely different. You met Gunter? He's terrific as Maxwell Koiner. Very hunky on the small screen. Is he short? Most of those actors are short."

I shrugged. "He's taller than me."

Nana's look said it all.

"Fine. He's tall—probably close to six feet."

"Where did you meet him? Is he really with Shep? I thought Shep had a thing with that artist friend of yours." She leaned to look at the article.

My nan is clever. She could ferret out a secret, from me in particular, so I was careful when I replied, "What...you don't believe this crap, do you? I didn't say they were together."

"Not together, together, but I can't imagine anyone else introducing you to an actor. You don't get out much."

"I get out plenty." It's sad when your grandmother has a more vibrant social life than you. I shoved the paper away. "This article doesn't make any sense. I had an accident. That's all."

"It's the *Post*, sweet pea, it doesn't need to make sense—they need to sell papers. Too bad they didn't mention Posh Nosh. That would be great publicity."

I scanned to the end. "Of all the pictures to choose...it's not like that reporter wasn't snapping a million photos yesterday morning." Nan gave me a questioning look. "I saw him after the accident—when I was uptown. Poppy and I have a gig at Shep's."

"How dreadful. Although you'll be hobnobbing with stars." Nan sipped her coffee and said astutely, "This reporter is after something—and he's thinking he can get it from you. He's applying pressure."

"I think so too." That dick. "He wants the scoop on closeted Shep McNamara, but that's yesterday's news."

"Maybe he wants something else. What are you going to do?"

"I'm going to make some phone calls."

"That doesn't sound at all vigorous."

"I'm not going to act rashly."

Nan cleared her throat.

"*I'm not.* I'll speak with Carrera and get my license back."

I had a few other things scheduled this morning—like breaking Carrera's nose with his camera—but I wasn't about to tell that to Nan. I glared at the paper. That fucker could have used a better shot. Why that one? And how the hell did he get his slimy hands on my license?

Cash. That's how. *Compensation,* he'd said. How did he know to go to Cappy's? It was likely he'd placed that tracking device on Gunter's car. I needed to call Dan.

I shoved the paper aside and slurped soggy cereal.

Nan sat with her rye toast and eyed me calmly. She spread raspberry jam with the back of her spoon, and I tried not to wince at her breakfast choice. When she set the spoon down, her voice was as sticky-sweet as her jam. "It's nice to see you this morning. Where's Dan?"

For the record, Dan and I do not have slumber parties here at Nan's, much to her disappointment.

"Working a case. Nan. I'll be gone most of the weekend. You're going to have to ask Mom to take you to the market. I have to go to the Soapies."

Nan stopped mid-chew. "*Get out!* Really? The Soapies?" Her blue eyes sparkled. "See, Poppy makes your life more interesting. Although, you need fun that doesn't include test-driving BMWs." She set her toast down and scratched under a curler. "What are you wearing? Because, sweetie, I just remembered, I think your grandfather's tux is still in a dry-cleaning bag in the hall closet!"

Oh no. "Uhm. I think Joey has—"

"Nonsense." Her chair scraped the linoleum and, lickety-split, she and her bracelets jangled away, Bella in hotfooted pursuit.

I sighed at the paper, poured another teaspoon of sugar on my now-unappealing breakfast and texted Dan. He was probably still sleeping in the cushy splendor of Chez Gay.

Nan reappeared within minutes tearing a yellowing dry-cleaning bag from my Grandpa Cooper's powder blue tuxedo. The jacket sported lapels so wide they looked like outstretched wings. The seams were edged in white piping. "Here it is. I knew

I hadn't donated it—this is a Bill Blass! He wore it to the CPA Association ball in '75, I think."

"Bill Blass?"

"No. Don't be fresh. Your grandfather." Nan held the garment by its hanger, turning it slowly so I wouldn't miss a stitch of its finery.

"Nan. I'm fine. Really."

"Nonsense. Try it on."

*Shit.*

At nine I stood on the sticky sidewalk facing Cappy's Luxury Auto Sales, and for the first time since a college walk of shame eight years ago, I was sporting a baseball hat and dark shades. Earlier, I'd been asked several times if I was the sleazy guy from the newspaper. The beemer-basher. And that was in my own neighborhood. I was forced to duck into the fresh market, and for twenty-five bucks I now looked like every other paparazzi-dodging idiot in the city.

Still. Only one person asked me for a cigarette on the train, and a couple coeds in Mary-Kate and Ashley inspired rags wanted to know if I was the guy who played Peter Petrelli. That was four fewer than yesterday, so maybe the hat and glasses were a good idea.

At Cappy's the beach balls drooped heavily on their thin wires and the colorful pennants hung lifelessly in the crushing humidity. It was early, but the service-department door was propped open in Cappy's vain attempt to cool Manhattan with its overworked a/c unit. My father would have had a seizure over that waste. A few preoccupied salesmen stood squinting at their cell phones. I didn't see Tommy Cappelletti or his ten-gallon hat.

I texted Dan again. His silence wasn't unusual—he was working. So, adjusting the strap on my messenger bag, I headed to the showroom.

The first person I saw? Dan's blond friend leaning indolently against the back wall near a cardboard cutout of an eighty thousand dollar SUV. Obviously the car held no appeal for me. The mechanic held a plastic clipboard, and he blanched when I entered the blissfully cool room. Recognition turned his smile of welcome into a frozen grimace of alarm.

I sometimes have that affect on people, but in this instance, I'm sure I looked equally pale. There was something about John I didn't trust.

Something other than his too-good looks and his too-easy way with Dan.

It was dim inside the building with my sunglasses on, and cold air condensed on the cheap lenses. It was likely Carrera was still on my tail, but I tucked my glasses into my bag anyway. I approached the mechanic. "Hey. How are you? Is Stew in?"

"Stew?" His confusion looked real, but it was key to remember that this guy wasn't just watching the door at Shep's apartment for ten bucks an hour. He'd been Dan's paid squealer—an informant—back when Dan was on the force. Squealing was something Romanos frowned on in principle and reacted poorly to in person, so I gave him my best faux Soprano's smile. If I were a couple inches taller and a foot wider, it might have made all the difference. I made do by jabbing two fingers in his direction.

"Someone gave my license to the paper. Someone from Cappy's. I was here yesterday—"

"I know. Who could forget? You saw the paper? Wow. Hey, we have a few extra copies here if you need one for your family—"

"Yes. I saw the paper," I snapped. Everyone in New York had seen the paper. "So." I made a firm slicing gesture with my left hand. "Last time I laid eyes on my I.D.? It was in the hands of your tattooed friend from the service department. Stew. Where is he?"

John's name, stitched in white on his cotton breast pocket, moved as he shrugged. "I'm sorry, but there's no one by that name here. Could you have given it to someone else?"

He was so...mild.

"Where's Cappelletti?"

"Tommy? He was let go after yesterday's incident."

My voice hiked an octave. "Let go? You mean fired?"

"This wasn't his first incident."

"So the big guy? Buzzed blond—tattoo that said *mother*—he's not here?"

"No. No Stew that I ever met. I'm the only blond in service or parts. You sure he worked here? There was quite a crowd yesterday."

"I—" There had been quite a crowd, actually. I only assumed Stew was an employee of Cappy's. He could have been someone off the street.

John nodded to another employee. He was eager to get to work, so I asked my next question. "Did a reporter come by here? Jorge Carrera? Big camera and a phony tail?"

The handsome mechanic's lips tightened and he said woodenly, "I don't speak with reporters. You tell Albright I said that. We have a code of conduct here—this is an exclusive dealership. We get all kinds of people—famous people. Movie-star types. We don't speak to reporters."

No. He only spoke to cops. "He was paying—offering cash."

John nodded toward the stylish receptionist. "Talk to Teresa. She might know where your license is. Man, you need to update your I.D. That mustache? That's what my old man called pencil thin."

I was sick of hearing about the mustache. I handed him my card—Pish Posh Nosh in pink script. John wasn't bowled over by Poppy's curlicue lettering. "Call me if Stew shows. I'd appreciate it."

He tucked my business card into his pocket and then tucked his clipboard under his armpit. His biceps flexed in the blue work shirt. John's slim waist was emphasized by oil-stained work Dickies and a worn leather belt. The mechanic was fit and firm and in his late twenties. Tall. Blond. His cologne was a manly combination of motor oil and cheap Axe deodorant. I wondered again if he and Dan shared a more intimate history.

Which was ridiculous of me. It was none of my business. I didn't have a free pass to judge Dan's past just because we were involved now. He had slept with other men, just as I had. And he had to put up with my former lover in the shape of Sheppard McNamara *Actor* for the next four blessed days. I couldn't possibly be upset.

Which meant that I was.

John nodded. "I'll let you know. If you see Albright, tell him I have something for him. He's not answering his phone."

No. He wasn't. What could I do but return his nod? "Sure. I'll pass the message along."

Fifteen minutes and one stilted conversation with the offended Teresa later, I wasn't any closer to getting my license returned. It wasn't on the premises—so I left Cappy's.

On my way to the train, I phoned Dan again—no voice mail. What kind of business was he running? I tried again, and this time he picked up.

"Hey."

"Dan Albright's phone, how may I direct your call?"

I literally stopped on the sidewalk and held my phone at arm's length. I stared at it before putting it back to my ear. "Uh. May I ask who this is?"

"Who is this please?"

"This is Caesar Romano."

"How may I direct your call?"

"You can direct me directly to Albright. Who the hell is this?"

"This is Stephen Taylor—Mr. Albright is unavailable. May I take a message?"

Why was Shep's twinky assistant answering Dan's phone? "Stephen. It's Caesar. We met yesterday morning. Where's Albright?"

"I'm sorry. Your name isn't ringing a bell. Would you—?"

"I'm the caterer." I ground my teeth. "Put. Albright. On."

"I'm sorry. He's unavailable and I'm taking his messages. May I ask who is calling?"

"Are you for real? Hang up the phone and let it go to voice mail." That idiot had the audacity to answer Dan's phone? Where the hell was he? I checked my watch—9:26. He should be working, sitting in his stinky car following leads on Kendal Schmidt and protecting green-eyed Gunter's endangered life.

I needed to get working myself.

I shut the phone on Shep's eccentric assistant and entered the subway, burrowing into the underground. You'd think it would be cooler, but you'd be wrong. The morning heat and the steady traffic of both sweaty pedestrians and overheated subway cars, mixed with the sickly sweet odor of old urine, made the tunnel noxious. Typical summer in the city.

I wasn't paying attention to my surroundings—something I wouldn't dare admit to a certain Staten Island PI—instead I texted Poppy and spoke briefly with my uncle Tino. My uncles were on board and thrilled. I was nervous but relieved. They'd swing by later.

"Tell me about the paper," Tino demanded.

"Gotta go! Trains coming!" I snapped my phone shut.

Woolgathering about what I yet had to do this morning, I found myself on the wrong side of the tracks.

I climbed the opposite stairs, crossed the pedestrian walk and righted my wrong.

There were only a few people waiting—most of them mothers with young children or sullen-looking college kids. A couple bums were curled against the wall. The train's approach rumbled through the soles of my shoes and, glancing from my phone, I looked casually across the tracks—and directly into the malicious stare of Stew the jug-headed blond who apparently didn't work for Cappy's Luxury Auto Sales. Three of his fingers were bandaged in silver splints—it looked like a home-repair job.

We stared at each other until Stew spat something on the ground, gum I hoped, and then he slunk along the platform's edge, moving with determination toward the pedestrian walk.

There was no way his presence here was a coincidence. Either that squealer John had called Stew, or this goon was following me. He looked pissed. Possibly that was just his face. No question now that Stew had given my license to the newspaperman. Why? Because I'd broken his fingers.

And that was no one's fault but his own.

Stew climbed the stairs, turning once to give me a malevolent smile, and my skin chilled in the dense air.

Up ahead in the darkened tunnel, a subway light flickered. The metal on metal shriek of the cars' brakes couldn't come quickly enough. Stew glared at me...and I was good to go.

I texted Dan, hoping that idiot Stephen wasn't deleting my texts, and Stew hit the pedestrian walk above us. He held me in his line of vision, and from the concrete overpass his eyes were hooded like those of a predator. I wasn't keen on becoming his prey. He pursed his lips, and from here? It looked like he was whistling.

*What a freak.*

I opted not to chat with him after all. He could keep my I.D.—it was too late to do more than regret anyway. It was time for a new license. I would head to Penn Station later and spend the rest of the day standing in line.

The train arrived and we pressed forward. The warning clanged and the doors popped open with a bang. Stew came purposefully down the stairs and I scrammed. I entered the car with a twist—which didn't feel too great, actually. I made my way to the back, dodging passengers and gingerly weaving my way to the doors at the far end of the car. *C'mon. C'mon. Close doors. Close.*

The doors gaped open an inordinately long time. They yawned wide, as if they were waiting.

On the platform, stumpy white hair flashed in the crowd and then Stew dipped into the far door on the subway car.

I'm not sure why, but I exited from my own set of doors onto the stained platform—just to see if Stew followed? Yes. Because when his flat eyes met my stare through the smeared window, the door alarm rang and the unsmiling Stew stepped on the subway platform.

I had a bad feeling about this.

I ducked back into the car and he did as well, the two of us now caught in a bizarre game of follow the leader—or cat and mouse. The door finally jerked to a close, and I exited the train with a neat, if stiff, turn.

Stew moved as well. He wasn't spry or quick. He was a lummox. The door snapped closed on his unlucky, previously uninjured fingers, and the man crumpled against the window. His yelp of pain reverberated through the subway station. His cheek met the filthy glass.

"Open it! Open the door!"

Fingers shuddered against the door seal, wriggling much as they had yesterday in the car window, and I bolted. Pandemonium erupted inside the subway car. They would stop the train—but before Stew could free himself, and heedless of my bruise, I leaped the stairs, flew through the turnstile and burst into the wall of heat and sunshine on the street.

The paparazzi were in place, loitering on the sidewalk outside Shep's. They sipped gallon-sized sodas, cameras at the ready, and waited fat and florid for someone to exploit. It was a bone-melting ninety-two degrees on the Island of Manhattan. The air was thick with garbage and bus fumes, and I was extra careful to avoid contact with anything sticky—railings, handles, parking meters—it was all gummy in the heat.

I tugged my hat, pushed my glasses and moved with the misguided confidence of the disguised. I wasn't exactly invisible, but I hoped I would fool the photographers.

Just short of Shep's tony building, Jorge Carrera materialized from the alleyway. "Mr. Romano—a minute of your time?"

I didn't miss a step. Jorge looked as if he'd been enjoying a morning inside the a/c as I sweltered on the cross-city bus. He was smooth and weirdly sweatless.

"Sure, but I get to ask the questions."

"We could have a little give and take?"

"No. You've already taken, haven't you?" He looked confused, so I enlightened him. "You took my photo and plastered it across every paper in New York. Haven't you ever heard of ethical journalism?"

"You're upset? There was nothing uncomplimentary—"

"You said I was twenty-nine, for starters."

"That must have been a typo."

"Look. I don't know you and I don't care one way or the other what you're up to, but leave my name out of your gossip column—unless you're promoting our catering service—and quit following me. You're creeping me out. I saw you last night. I don't know what you need, but I have work to do."

Carrera shrugged. "It's a free country. If you have nothing to hide, you should be fine. Are you worried?"

"About? I just want my license back."

"Are you sure? Because I don't have it with me."

"Fine. Buzz off."

That surprised him. He must be accustomed to paying people to spill all kinds of idiotic drivel about themselves. I didn't need to pay people to listen to me—and besides, I had nothing of interest to say. Jorge tried one last time, "Wait. Maybe we can help each other."

I shook his hand from my sleeve. It hadn't been the greatest morning ever and my patience had tanked. I said with finality, "Touch me again and I'll have you arrested."

I ditched the flabbergasted Carrera at the curb and climbed the steps to Shep's building. Time to go to work, but first—I had to run the paparazzi gauntlet.

"Mr. Romano—"

"Mr. Romano—"

"Caesar, can I have a minute—"

Camera shutters went *click click click* inches from my face and I tugged my hat lower. Holy hell. I was famous.

# Chapter Eight:
# Short Term

Stephen Taylor answered the unguarded door on the fifteenth floor. That lack of security was my first clue that Dan was in the apartment. He was holding down the fort.

"May I help you?" Stephen sniffed.

I brushed past him and dropped my messenger bag on the Persian rug. The Muzak was gone. In its place, German pop music pulsed from behind the kitchen door. I didn't understand a word, but it was spunky and thick with consonants.

Still, it was pleasant inside the apartment—the very antithesis of the grimy gossip scene at street level. A cool, comfortable sixty-five degrees eased my mood, and for the first time in memory, I was happy to be at Shep's. The entry was cheerful, bright and stringently clean...and there was a trace of cigarette smoke in the air. Gunter was disregarding the house rules. Why that put a fresh smile on my face, I didn't know.

"Excuse me. Do you have an appointment?" Stephen closed the door and blinked at me expectantly. "Mr. McNamara is unavailable, perhaps you could come by later?"

I dropped my hat on the hall table. "Has Poppy arrived?"

"The caterer? Pish Posh? She's...on her way, I understand. She phoned..." He checked his handheld device as I checked the mirror. For a man who had two car accidents yesterday, I looked all right. "It's roughly ten minutes until she's scheduled. Are you with the caterer?"

I quit fluffing my pathetically ridged hat hair and turned to consider Shep's strange new assistant. He stared back, his expression careful. I said with exaggerated care, as if he were impaired, "Stephen. We met *yesterday*. Do you have a problem with me?"

Stephen shook his head and offered me a nervous smile. Today the forgetful youngster wore a canary yellow and pale pink Argyll polo shirt and a pair of pressed charcoal-striped trousers. He had a whip-thin belt—the little fashion bug. "No-no-no problem." He retrieved my bag and hat and set them together in the closet. "I...remember..."

"Good. I'm here to work. Poppy should be arriving with some of our staff to help unload the van." First trip of many. I had doubled up on Motrin so I was set for the afternoon. "If you'll excuse me...is Dan here?" I had a lot to tell him.

"Dan. Dan. There are many Dans in New York City..." The music spiked from behind the kitchen door, and Stephen muttered, "That man."

"Is that Gunter? I like this music. It suits him." I hit the swinging door to Shep's restaurant-quality kitchen and was brought short by the sight of my wet-headed boyfriend lounging shirtless against the counter. His black hair was slicked away from his broad forehead. His jeans rode dangerously low on his hips. One hand gripped the counter, giving me a clear view of the scars striping his ribs and his right shoulder and the dark hair swirling his pecs. He looked delectable. He sipped absently from a red and white *Days* mug (this vision seared into my memory in a flash) as he watched—

—a tiger-striped-bikini-underwear-clad Gunter Heidelbach

run a razor over his lathered inner thigh. His left foot was high on the granite countertop while he chattered, "...and she left her filthy DVD in the computer where I couldn't help but to watch it!"

He was ridding himself of body hair in the kitchen sink under Dan's attentive gaze.

Like a mute fool I stood riveted inside the threshold. The door banged the wall and swung back, nearly smacking me in my stupefied face. Maybe it would knock some sense into me.

Gunter and Dan both jumped. Dan snapped to attention, his back stiffening like a marionette whose string had been yanked taut. His hand splayed above his six-pack, scars spread over the scars, and his dark eyes widened guiltily.

He said nothing.

Well. If that wasn't unsettling, I really didn't know what was.

But Gunter smiled in welcome. "Oh it's your little luff. *Guten Tag, Schatz.*"

*Little luff.*

The razor scraped to his pubic area, and Gun knocked the suds into the sink with a metallic *ting.* Health-code violation right there—I had to prep food in that sink tomorrow. Gun said needlessly, "I'm neatening for the party."

My expression must be telling because Dan swore under his breath.

Gunter pulled his head out of his ass enough to see the tension that vibrated between Dan and I. "What? I cannot leave the apartment for my appointment."

"I...actually...I...I..." Not only was cognitive thinking beyond my ability, coherent speech seemed to be out of reach as well. Shock had stifled my larynx. What the hell was Gunter doing? I mean other than the obvious. And...why was Dan watching him do it? It wasn't indignation holding me—it was something deeper.

I was hurt.

"Breathe, Ce. He's not shaving his ass."

I wet my lips and blinked at Dan.

Gunter chatted, "I want to be tidy for my win on Saturday. We'll hit the clubs late. I want to dance, yes? Party? You ah Italian—you know how it is to be robust and a bit hairy."

I looked from Dan to Gunter, and then from Gunter back to Dan. What had I walked in on? What had I come here for anyway? Why in the world was I here?

Work.

I was supposed to be working.

I found my voice along with my pride. "Don't you people have jobs?" and then I made my exit, slapping the door with enough force it smacked Stephen right in his iPhone, which unfortunately took flight. It sailed from his hand, then skittered across Shep's polished floor. That was too bad for Stephen, because by the looks of things, his brain functioned only with tech support.

I had to leave. I was doing all these people favors—Shep, Poppy, Dan, Gunter—and for what? Hassle. That's what. Poppy could direct the minions today. There was more than enough at Posh Nosh to keep me busy. I could sit down and maybe I could untape my chest, just for starters.

What I really needed was a cupcake. That's what I'd do. Get a nice cupcake, I'd untape my chest—and I still needed to go uptown to get my new license.

*Jesus Christ.* I was nearly dizzy with anger.

I stalked to the foyer, Dan close on my heels. "Ce. Wait."

I shook his hand from my shoulder. “Please don’t tell me to calm down right now. So help me—”

“Can I say please don’t be upset? Because you have no reason to be.”

“No. You may not. I’ve had a very trying morning and seeing Gunter’s privates—which I couldn’t help but notice you were admiring—didn’t make it any better. Aren’t you supposed to be following leads? Where’s your Johnny-on-the-spot at the door? Isn’t Kendal around here somewhere?”

“I’ve been working since five. I sat in the car for two stinking hours outside her ex’s apartment and...it was a little close in the car. I came back to take a shower and find someone to watch the door. I’m short-handed. I walked in about thirty minutes ago.”

I kept my vision clear of Dan, determined to get my bag and leave. I wrenched open the hall closet and hissed through my teeth as pain seared my chest. It shouldn’t hurt this bad, should it? I took six stupid Motrin. Six. Maybe I had broken a rib.

“Wait.”

I did wait, finally looking at him. “Where’s your cell?”

“What?” His voice changed. “What’s the real problem, Caesar? What’s this about?” It was subtle, but there was an edge. “I’m not going to defend myself over whatever you think I did. He was shaving his legs. That’s not my bag, and you know it.”

I’d give him that. I knew that somehow all this would be funny. Maybe a half hour from now—maybe an hour.

“You are my bag.” Dan’s voice was firm. “My phone died this morning. It’s charging on the table...” He glanced at the barren hall table. “What the hell? It was right there.”

"Stephen's been fielding your calls."

Dan scowled at Shep's employee. "Are you for real?"

"Mr. Albright. I took the liberty of answering your phone while you were indisposed in the shower. I haven't touched it since." The twink shook his own phone limply. "I took notes..."

Dan swore under his breath. I asked, "Did you see the paper this morning?"

"Yes, and that Carrera is walking a thin line as far as I'm concerned. Did you see him today?"

"He's hovering on the sidewalk right now." I wasn't going to withhold information from Dan just because I was angry. That would make me as much of an asshole as everyone else in the apartment. "Listen. You should know this before I go. Someone else is following me." I found my ball cap and my satchel.

"What? When? Who?" The sight of my butch new hat didn't deter Dan. I took a second to hide behind my new shades and then I described Stew. "That sounds like Lester Finch. Where did you see him? Hell, I looked for him all morning—credit report and police records. I called his parents. And he's with you? How the fuck do you do that?"

I threw my hands in the air. "Do what? That man was at Cappy's yesterday. If you were looking for him, *you could have mentioned it.* How could you possibly miss him?"

"You were distracting me." He bit those words out one by one. "Finch was Kendal's boyfriend."

I dropped my hands. "No way. He followed me into the subway not thirty minutes ago. Kendal was seeing him?"

"He worked for *Days*—that's how they met—but he was fired."

"Lot of that going around. Are you saying Gunter slept with that man?" My voice turned prudish. "That's disgusting."

"I didn't say he slept with him, I said the man made a pass at Gun."

"I don't believe it."

"Belief it!" Gun called from the hallway. He had his hands full calming the frazzled Stephen, who was now nearly hysterical over what I presumed was a broken cell. It was just a phone—the guy needed to get a grip.

Dan was all business. "I need to speak with your photographer."

"Fine. I'm sure the two of you will have a very illuminating conversation. Maybe *you should get dressed first.* I have it on good authority that people put their clothes on before business meetings." Apparently, I was still a little touchy. "I gotta go."

The thing is, I hate getting this angry. I hate it more when anyone sees it, Dan in particular. He might find my jealousy *feisty*, but I found it unprecedented and acutely embarrassing. I wasn't the jealous type, or so I'd come to believe, because jealousy boiled down to one thing. Insecurity.

And that was *so* unattractive.

Gunter butted in, "Oh no! Tell me you're not angry." Hard to listen to a man who had shaving cream hanging from his balls.

Dan's hand stopped me a second time. "Ce. I'll drive you. Quit glaring. I didn't do anything."

"I understand that, but I'm uncomfortable. You acted guilty."

"You surprised me."

"It didn't look like it was a nice surprise."

Stephen disappeared down the hall, and Gunter said, "I am sorry you are upset." It wasn't clear who that was aimed toward.

"Sure. You need to put some lotion on your legs or you're going to get a rash." Not that I knew from previous experience.

My lame parting shot was foiled as soon as I jerked the front door open. Poppy, decked in fetching periwinkle blue, stood blinking in the hallway, her hand poised to knock. Her dress matched her eyes perfectly, and her platinum hair fell like white silk to her shoulders. She held a red-and-purple paisley-covered gift box—an amber satin bow was tied elegantly on the top. She managed to be fresh as a daisy despite the heat. Poppy grinned at me and laughed. "Hey, Guido, you're famous."

At least someone thought I was a pleasant surprise. "I should have shaved that stupid mustache when you told me to."

"Told ya."

"Poppy." Dan weaseled to position himself in the doorway and stepped to block her view. His broad shoulders filled the entry. He placed one hand casually on the frame, and said suavely, "Hey. How are you?"

Poppy didn't blink. "What the hell is wrong with you?"

My heart swelled with love for my best friend. Dan was so confident in his ability to manipulate people—I watched him do this all the time—allowed him to do it to me. His surprise at her don't-fuck-with-me attitude gave me a thrill of satisfaction. My Poppy wasn't easily led.

She peered around Dan's chest, her brow furrowed. "Uh. You're blocking the door, Dan-a-rooni. I'm here to work. Get out of my way."

Dan glanced over his shoulder to where Stephen had reappeared. He had a different phone—a backup? Who had a backup? Gunter waited by the young assistant's side and smiled encouragingly at us. His tiger underwear bulged. I found myself staring at his package because, I had to admit, he was impressive. I snapped my gaze to Dan, who smirked back at me. "See?"

"Oh, shut up."

Gunter called, "Hello." He waved to Poppy.

"What the hell? Could you move?" Poppy said. "I need to tinkle."

Dan sighed. "Fine. Come in. But we need to tell you something first."

"We?" I asked.

"We," Dan said. Poppy was one step inside the apartment before she zeroed-in on the naked German. She gasped as Dan uselessly tried to warn her. "You need to be quiet about this, Poppy, because—"

"*Oh my God*," she squealed, "*It's Gunter Heidelbach! The soap star! I love you!*" Just in case we weren't privy to all those facts. I shook my head to clear it. My usually blasé partner smacked the gift box into Dan's stomach, and she blew in like a hurricane, cussing at me first. "You dick. Why didn't you tell me? I'd have told you."

"I was going to say something..."

Dan shut the front door. "Gun, this is Poppy McNamara. Shep's cousin."

"Ah," he cooed, "you look exactly like Sheppard, only far prettier." Just like Shep, Gunter somehow made greeting a stranger while standing in his knickers an art form. Maybe they learned this in acting school. Exhibitionism 101.

I had to give her credit—Poppy's gaze strayed low once and then she kept her attention square on Gunter's apple-green eyes.

Gunter flirted outrageously while Poppy blushed and giggled like a schoolgirl. The sly actor took her hand in that double grip he'd employed on me yesterday, only she didn't try to pull away. She leaned into him. Good Lord, he was reeling her in. The fucker probably acquired that trick in acting school too.

Dan checked the gift box. "What's this?"

Poppy said, without taking her boobs from Gunter's arm, "The doorman asked me to bring it up. Special delivery for Shep's guest. That's Gunter, right? Shep's guest? I can't believe no one told me. I thought the doorman meant Caesar." She giggled again.

"Me? Why would anyone send me a gift here?"

Dan pondered the box. "Maybe Carrera is wooing you."

"Mmm. Maybe." I took the box from Dan. "I should open it then, don't you think?" I asked sweetly.

Stephen wrestled the package from me. "I'm Mr. McNamara's assistant. I'll handle this."

Dan laid a big, firm hand on Stephen's thin shoulder. "I'll take that."

Without a word, Shep's dapper assistant handed the box to Dan as Gun led a willing Poppy by the hand into the foyer. "Maybe that is for me." He didn't sound flirty now. His words were tinged with concern and small lines appeared on his brow. "I am the guest."

Dan said, "I think so. There's no tag, but I'll assume this is for you." The air vibrated now. There was an edge that hadn't existed, even when I was angry. Dan and Gun exchanged a look I could easily interpret. This was suspicious. And, call me crazy, but that gift wrap smacked of Kendal Schmidt's house of style.

Dan popped the lid off the box. "What time was your appointment this morning, Gun?"

"Appointment?"

"Wax. Manscape. Trim. Whatever you call it."

Poppy finally glanced at Gunter's underwear.

"Quarter past ten. Why?"

I looked at my watch—10:25. Less than an hour since I'd seen Stew.

"Kendal make that appointment for you?"

"Yes. She was my assistant." Gunter nodded toward the ineffectual Stephen. "It's what they do."

"Well. Someone knows where you are, and pretty much they know what you're doing." Dan extracted a disposable razor from the depth of the striped box.

We all stared until Stephen joined us and, looking at me, he said, "Excuse me. Do you have an appointment?"

Twenty minutes later the three of us glided through midday traffic on our way to Rockefeller Center. Me. My boyfriend. And renowned soap opera star, Gunter Heidelbach. He'd hastily thrown on some pricy True Religion jeans and T-shirt (both of which I coveted immediately) and, in a basic black ball cap and wickedly expensive ice-blue John Lennon styled sunglasses, he still looked exactly like Gunter Heidelbach, Soap Star.

I kept my mouth shut for a variety of reasons, the spoiled chicken not the least of them. A dozen Christmas tree air fresheners couldn't mask the intense fragrance permeating everything in the car—even with all four windows down. This was why Dan had chosen a midmorning shower.

Good call.

"We should haff taken my carh," Gunter whined for the fifteenth time. He hung from the passenger window, sandy hair blowing around his cute little ears. He was attempting to smoke a Marlboro, and about to lose his hat.

"Get your head in the fucking car before someone sees you," Dan said for the fifteenth time. "And put that thing out."

"It makes the carh smell better."

"Oh, you can't argue with that." I tugged my own hat low, convinced that someone was following us at this very moment. We'd been discreet in our back alley exodus, and I hadn't seen Carrera, but that didn't mean he wasn't hot on our scent. I mean it'd be kind of hard to miss it.

"You have so much crap back here." Gun was crammed beside Dan's PI paraphernalia—a camera bag, notebooks, a cooler. I tried not to think about what was festering in the upholstery.

"Where's your laptop?" His saddlebag was absent.

"At Shep's. I'm working in the back bedroom." I knew precisely which bedroom he meant. Dan handed me a stick of spearmint gum, which I took. I considered it a peace offering. Gun snagged a piece as well, and I was horrified when he pitched the cigarette through the open window. Dan didn't even blink, but his knuckles whitened on the wheel. He said to me, "What do you think?"

"Of? I think Kendal's boyfriend is a knuckle-dragging lunatic. He scared the shit out of me, but he's not smart enough to play games with either you or Gun. Why didn't you call the police?"

"Gun received a gift. He's an actor—people send him crap all the time."

"Quite right. In the past, I let my secretaries handle my packages." Gunter's blond brows wiggled suggestively above the thin frames of his designer glasses, and I almost laughed.

Dan snapped his gum. "Seriously, the police can do nothing. This is why Gun hired me. What happened to you this morning?"

"Stew, excuse me, *Lester Finch*—Jesus. What the heck kind of name is that anyway? It has to be an alias."

"Nope."

"Well, Lester and Carrera are both following me. I think someone has residual rage left over from Cappy's. His hand was banged up." I described the fingers to Dan.

Gun tossed, "Serfs him right. He's vile."

"Yes, well, be that as it may, I don't understand why Finch pursued me this morning. I mean other than the finger ac—cident." I stumbled, remembering the subway door closing on the fingers of his good hand. I cleared my throat. "I never saw that man before yesterday. If he's pissed at Gun, shouldn't he be—*ooohh.* You mean Stew is your GPS guy." I looked at Gun. "So he made a pass at you, you told Kendal, Kendal freaked and blamed you—"

"I do bring out the beast in some men."

"Gun." Dan sounded annoyed, and I knew that spending time with Gunter was wearing on him.

"So you fired Kendal, and Finch got dumped—he was tracking your car because you're the cause of his misery? It certainly fits his thug personality profile."

Dan nodded. "Probably. If he was at Cappy's, then yeah, he was tracking the BMW—I had Gun leave the car with my guy to be serviced."

*My guy.* "Aren't those things illegal?"

"Yup."

"But...but...what about Kendal? Did she send the razor or did Lester?" Actually, Lester Finch was probably spending his day at the closest Intermediate Care Facility. It would be tricky to bandage one injured hand with the other. I'd had a hard enough time taping my own ribs. "Why would that creep give a reporter my driver's license? Other than for money. There's no sound reason. Jorge Carrera wasn't even at Cappy's when I had my accident."

"Accidents," Dan corrected.

"Right. That car accident happened before I ever crossed paths with Carrera."

I was using the word *accident* a lot.

Dan said. "Maybe—"

Gunter piped in, "Jorge Carrera is a parasite. He is after my story. Any story. Every story. He is a louse. It's most disconcerting."

"But why would Lester Finch give him *my* license?"

"It is a terrible photo," Gunter offered from the backseat. "I would sue."

"Thank you. That's helpful."

"I'm sorry." Gunter flopped back against the seat. He stared at the scenery from his open window and bit his lip worriedly. "I haff an important interview today and I am uncomfortable to be out uf the apartment—someone wants to hurt me. You ah still attractive in my eyes, although facial hair doesn't suit you."

"So everyone tells me," I said through my teeth. I asked Dan, "Why do I matter to any of these people?"

"Are you done?" Dan asked.

"Not really, but go ahead." It must be a hundred degrees in the car. My shirt had sweat-glued me to the seat. I mopped the back of my neck with my collar and stared at the scaffolding embracing St. Patrick's Cathedral. The sidewalk was congested with pedestrians. On the steps, a bum with a leashed parrot smiled for two Asian men with cameras.

Dan said, "You're right in assuming that Lester's on to you because of the car. If he was tracking Gun's car, it brought him to the lot—which was my intention. I'm not clear if Finch is looking for Schmidt—their breakup didn't go well, she could be hiding from him—or if he's assisting her. He's pretty devoted."

"Like a dog," Gunter added.

"Either way, Carrera is nosy, and I'm sure he contacted Finch. He contacts everyone—it's his job. Carrera must have shown Finch your picture. You're on their radar now."

"If you hurt Finch, as you say..." Gun's manicured hands reached to grip the headrest passionately, "...that creature will hunt you. He's an animal. Please take care."

I was a little worried now—because I'd injured him twice. "Gun. If you wounded his pride, you're in danger too."

Gun said, "I belief you are correct that Kendal is the real aim for the reporter. And through her, me. He is looking for an angle."

Kendal had been Gun's assistant for an entire year. As a former assistant myself, I'd learned far more about my boss than had been comfortable for either of us. I supposed if I were desperate enough, and pissed as well as unethical, I could be swayed to sell those secrets. If Kendal was angry enough to be bought, then Carrera was going after her with cash in hand. "Does Kendal have something on you?"

Dan checked the rearview mirror, and Gun's blue lenses met his look.

Okay, then. Someone had something to hide.

"She's here in the city—somewhere." Dan hit the blinker and made a right onto 48th Street. The road and both sidewalks bustled with midday visitors, some of them sunburned. "Caesar, remember the plan—I'm going to double-park and you take the wheel."

"Just like Jesus."

Dan didn't budge. "Circle the block once or twice and meet me back here. I'll text you." He threw the car in park, checked the rearview mirror again and unbuckled his seat belt. "I have someone escorting Gun back to the apartment."

"An escort? Why does that sound illegal?" I was not about to second-guess him in front of a client, but I did wonder why he was leaving that particular job to a minion. Presumably, Dan knew his shit. Who was I to ask questions about security? "Fine."

He softened a little. "I know you have work to do. I appreciate this."

"Please make it quick. That wretched party is tomorrow night."

"As if any one of us could forget." He sighed and leaned to peck my cheek. "Cheer up, Ce. You get to meet my parents this weekend."

"Huh? How can we still—"

"I moved it to Sunday." He smiled like he'd given me a slice of birthday cake.

I smiled back like I was allergic to wheat.

He and Gun hopped from the car, both doors slamming. Now was not the time to mention taking another rain check on meeting his parents. But where would he stash Gun while we had tea and crumpets at Westchester Manor? He'd probably take the engaging German with us. Maybe Gunter could play the role of Caesar Romano in the "let's go meet Dan's parents" scene? He'd do a fabulous job.

I climbed into the driver's seat, and Gunter startled me when he leaned into the window. Flashing his zillion-dollar smile, he kissed my cheeks as only Europeans do—*kiss kiss*—and then he fumbled in his jeans for his pack of smokes. I wanted to put a bag over his head, he was so damn obvious.

"*Danke*, Caesar. You have been gracious and I am distressed about ah earlier mix up. I don't wish to offend you. Ah you angry?"

He was so...straightforward. Despite the littering, the outrageous flirting, the searching hand on the flowery couch and the recent crotch-shaving incident, Gunter was rapidly growing on me. It could be his sincerity, or possibly his accent, but I thought it was his zest. And according to everyone I knew, life could always use a bit more zest.

Gunter would make a fun friend, as long as he kept his grabby hands and his smooth thighs to himself.

I gave him an encouraging smile. "No, but I appreciate you asking. Now get the hell inside, and stay out of trouble. Pull your hat down. Good luck with the interview."

He lit his cigarette, and those damn glasses sparkled iridescent blue. "I will slay them."

"Shake a leg, man." Dan's shades mirrored the crowd. He was all business, as was appropriate. "You're making yourself a target."

I let pedestrians cross while Dan and Gun navigated their way through Rockefeller Plaza. At midday, the sun was unrelenting and in spite of the heat the courtyard was crowded with tourists. Every available spot was filled—lunch bags were open and pigeons fought for crumbs. I sweltered in the car and stared longingly at the hotdog cart. A cold Perrier would really hit the spot.

I still wanted a cupcake. More precisely, I craved a red velvet cupcake with cream-cheese frosting. Poppy had some in the bakery case and they were going to be mine.

Dan and Gunter vanished easily through the revolving door, and I put the Camry into drive, cautiously heading to the next set of traffic lights. A sea of people dressed in summer clothes, work clothes, business suits and costly apparel flowed like the tide around the creeping Camry. I couldn't go any faster without nicking some poor visiting dentist from Duluth, and I was *not* using the word *accident* ever again.

Also, I was technically driving without a license.

Tourists snapped photos in front of the towering building. On the corner, next to the NBC store, a uniformed security guard casually conversed with a man dressed as a circus clown. That only heightened my opinion that people were crazy and no one in New York cared. Every make and model of humanity converged here at Rockefeller Center. It was a hub of Manhattan, and so different from Brooklyn, or even the Village. Faces blended into the crowd. From the lowest end of the social spectrum to the very highest—unless you were Donald Trump himself—you were anonymous. Unnoticed. With the possible exception of clowns and men in chicken suits—and in that case, people dismissed you.

Stew or Jorge or even Kendal could stop to feed the pigeons ten feet away and I wouldn't differentiate them from the rest of the crowd—I'd gloss over them.

I drove to the light, allowing plenty of distance between me and the next car. One might say there was too much distance, but one couldn't be too careful. A taxi nearly clipped me, urging me to move forward with the blare of his horn and an insistent nudge to the bumper, but I stayed put.

I stayed put and Kendal Schmidt entered the crosswalk dressed as a miniature midtown police officer. Her cayenne-pepper hair was held in a ponytail beneath an ugly blue hat—not that I was anyone to judge in my own dime-store ball cap—and she sailed past the bumper of the car in front of me without a by-your-leave. She all but swung a nightstick and whistled, she was that casual.

*I never would have seen her.*

I laid on the horn. It was the only thing I could think to do, and Kendal jerked. She gave the car a cursory look, but with the sun glinting off the windshield, she probably couldn't see me. Even if she could glean me through my *disguise*, the woman had no idea who I was.

"Kendal! Kendal, wait." She looked once. Her eyes were greener than I expected. That splash of freckles was unmistakable—splotches of brown pigment covered the bridge of her nose and rode the length of her cheekbones. She didn't waste another second. She picked up her tiny feet and moved through the crosswalk with more juice than she'd started with.

Obviously, I couldn't follow. The street was stuffed with pedestrians and the light glowed a nonnegotiable red. Not that I would ever run a traffic light, not even for someone impersonating a police officer. I sat in the car, taxis beeping and bumping me from behind, and Kendal darted dangerously through the 6th Avenue traffic. She was aimed toward the subway station.

A tour bus blocked my view and I lost her. I stewed in the curry-mobile until the freaking light changed, then I crept the slow creep across the intersection, sucking exhaust and tainted Thai food and angling to catch a glimpse of that fiery hair. Once I found her, I promptly lost her again as she sank down the cement steps to the subway station.

She was gone.

# Chapter Nine: Monkey Suit

Dan Albright waited on the sidewalk in front of Godiva Chocolatier. It looked like he'd run a hand through his hair a few times too many. It stuck in thick clumps, but it made him more ruggedly handsome. I noted he didn't come bearing chocolates, which was too bad. After everything I'd been through, I deserved chocolate.

He jerked the driver door open, did a quick double take over his shoulder and said, "Scoot. Did you really see her?"

I scooted. He sounded preoccupied. "I texted you as much. Yes. Red hair. Freckles. A munchkin. It's her. Unmistakable. She's dressed as a cop, and she took the subway heading downtown. I would have followed her, but I was *driving.*"

"Followed her? Are you delirious?"

"Well, I have been basting in salmonella fumes...but no."

"Ce. No following anyone. I don't mind you tagging along—"

"Tagging along? Hello? I think you're dragging me along."

"—or watching the door, but don't...do anything rash."

"Rash?" I bristled. "I'm never rash. I don't go in with guns blazing—things just happen around me and I react."

"Fine. Don't *react* without me—you've done that before.

This case is more delicate than you know."

"Meaning I don't have the whole story."

"You're absolutely sure it was her?"

A non-answer from Dan is very much an answer, so I let it slide. "Yes. I called her by name and she bolted into traffic. It was Kendal Schmidt. She looked right at me. Well, she looked right through me."

"At least we know she's here and that she's alive."

*"Alive?* Was there any question?"

"There's always a question."

"That's rather dark."

"I've been around the block. Sometimes things end pretty fucking badly." His voice was tight.

"Should I be worried that I'm being targeted by the creepy ex?"

"I don't think so. He doesn't have a record. No history of violence. Not even a traffic violation. He looks worse than he is."

"I find that impossible to believe."

"It was Kendal who threatened Gunter. That's a fact, Caesar. So don't do anything hasty. Lester Finch was humiliated by Gun and dumped by Kendal and fired by the studio—he's had a hard week. The accident"—again with that word—"shouldn't be too high on his list of priorities."

Easy for him to say. He hadn't seen Lester's fingers.

Dan maneuvered the car into an unlikely opening in traffic—a bit fast for my taste—and we headed speedily toward the job I was eons late for.

We zipped the length of one block and caught the tail end of the light.

"You can slow down if you like. Poppy and Andre are back

with the van. I have a few minutes." A tiny, tiny white lie, but I was gripping the dash with both hands as we left taxis behind us in the smog. Dan bombed down Fifth Avenue, cutting expertly between cars and delivery trucks. This was cop driving. Intense, focused, determined cop driving. I waited for him to slap one of those *Starsky and Hutch* sirens on the roof.

"We're fine."

"If you say so, but that lady and her dog just long-jumped the crosswalk."

"Relax."

I pried my nails from the dash and checked the security of my seat belt. The strap sliced into my aching ribs, but I was cleared for liftoff. "So. Your turn. How did it go with Gun?"

"Fine."

"These one-word answers don't cut it, Albright. Speak. You think Kendal was waiting for Gun at NBC? She was on the same block. That's not coincidental."

"He and Estelle arranged the interview this morning. She couldn't have known. It's the only reason I agreed to take him."

He was quiet and I could nearly see the wheels turning. He was keeping a lot from me—which was fine. His job required secrets. It was fine.

Really.

"The cop thing bothers me." He grunted. "She could have been watching him the entire time."

Dan's driving verged on reckless—or maybe not. Maybe I was unprepared for offensive driving—I was solidly on the defensive team. Maybe he was just hurrying, but an alarming breeze was blowing through the car. "Are you late for something?"

"Not yet, but I will be."

I inhaled sharply as he swerved around a bike messenger, and my regret was instantaneous. I didn't know which was worse, the pain in my lungs or the smell in my head. I stuck my nose out of the window and fought for cleanish air. "Jesus. You need to find a different car. It's getting worse, even with this cross ventilation."

"Working on it." He inched through the narrow space between two buses, and I pulled my face into the relative safety of the car. He didn't notice, he was too busy doubting me. "You're absolutely, positively sure that was Kendal? There are a lot of redheads in the city."

"Yes. What is this, sixth grade? I'm sorry it's not the answer you're looking for, but I pinkie promise it was her. Cross my heart." I kept busy identifying all the possible projectiles in our path. We were traveling now at warp speed. My stomach rolled, all thoughts of cupcakes and Godiva chocolate replaced by a more urgent need for Pepto-Bismol and ginger ale. Not to whine, but I was getting carsick.

I'd keep that information to myself.

Dan rounded a corner, and I looked disbelievingly at the geography. We were at NYU. Not five minutes had ticked by. "How the hell did you do that?"

"I'm experienced." He said this without a wink, nod, nudge, grope or any other indication that his words were laced with sexual innuendo.

I huffed the fresh air flowing crazily past my window. "So...we're heading to Posh Nosh, yeah?"

Dan made another right, no signal, two wheels, my hand cradling my side, and this time he pulled onto Christopher Street.

Quiet, beautiful, historic, totally-not-where-we-were-headed Christopher Street.

"You, uh, missed the turn."

He nodded. "I know. I need to make a quick stop."

"Fine, because no kidding, as much as I have a job I'd like to keep, I want nothing more than to get out of this car."

At last, Dan glanced at me. "Oh. Hey. You okay? You look a little green."

"Now you notice? I'm fine. Really." I needed to man the fuck up.

He drove us through one last intersection, nice and easy, and we came to a halt at a thirty dollar per day parking lot. I'd pony that money up myself if it meant I could flee the Camry.

"Here's the plan."

"Plan?" I asked from the sidewalk. "Today we have a plan?"

The car chirped as Dan set the alarm. He came around the hood and tossed the keys to the attendant. We were just down the street from the Stonewall Inn. A line of sweaty tourists waited in the park to have a photo taken in front of the Segal.

Dan joined me. His shades were on and he was all business. "I can use your help."

"Sure." My help? "You want me to canvas the neighborhood for Schmidt? Maybe she went back to her apartment." We were fairly close. We could stop in and water her African Violets.

"Not quite. I have Kendal's apartment covered."

That was mysterious, but I wasn't about to ask.

It was boiling hot on the sidewalk, but Dan's shirt managed to look crisp. He wore a handsome pair of black loafers today, no biker boots, and except for the fact that he was remarkably good-looking, he was just another New Yorker. Jeans and a tailored Egyptian cotton button-down, sleeves rolled sexily to the elbow. He'd done something to his hair in the last few minutes—smoothed it. He moved in a loose gait, ambling down the sidewalk. The frenetic pace of only a few minutes ago…where had that gone? He had slipped into some new character. Such a chameleon, my man Dan. Who was he really?

I kept the easy pace. It felt good to stretch my legs.

"Have you ever been to Zippos?" Dan pressed the button at the crosswalk and we waited for the light.

"Costume Emporium? Sure. They rent for Halloween."

"Yeah. They also offer large-scale rentals for local theatres—and they rent to the TV studios. They build some costumes, they tailor and they have a line in with some of the soaps. Like *Days*. Kendal worked for Zippos."

Zippos was one of those landmarks in New York City that you could easily pass without ever noticing. Behind the tacky street-level storefront crouched a massive red brick warehouse. The faded paint of last century's advertising still showed on the red brick bordering the alley. Giant second- and third-story windows faced the street. Inside, the entire building was overstuffed with dusty costumes and worn theatrical supplies.

"I remember the magnet. That's neat and tidy." And only three blocks from her apartment. "She must have been thrilled to land that job with Gun."

Some people do enjoy the notoriety that surrounded celebrities. Even minor ones. Not that there was anything minor about Gunter—to be fair, it would have been fun to be his assistant, although one would have their hands pretty full. Especially if one was gay and young and good-looking. Gun would be all over that. He'd dig the power play. Those flashy, long-lashed eyes would coax and wink and flutter—and then *bam* he'd be bending you over the nearest furnishing. I had no trouble imagining Gunter chasing some frantic secretary around the desk. A male secretary.

Someone like Stephen Taylor. He was the right combination

of prim, dapper, adoring and stupid.

Gunter would definitely hit that.

Dan's voice called me from my musing. "Estelle got Kendal the job."

"You said." Estelle Rosenstein, the woman with big teeth, big jewelry, a crass laugh and a brutal handshake. She was a top agent in New York and a force of nature. Estelle had found Stephen his job too. That was her job, I guess, to find other people jobs. I glanced at Dan. She'd hooked Detective Dan up with the residents of Chez Gay as well. "Lot of that going around. Kendal must have felt like the shop girl who hit the big time."

"By all accounts she did. Until last weekend when she went loco."

We arrived. The plain sign on the door announced that Zippos had wheeled and dealed in costume and fripperies since 1981.The year I was born. Almost thirty years of selling fat suits and top hats. That had to wear.

"Here's the drill. You're a fussy costume designer—"

"Oh, please."

"And I'm Dan Green."

I couldn't help it. I smiled. "Again with the Green?"

"Always." Dan's finger touched my wrist and a bolt of lightning scrambled my thoughts. His voice was husky. "You used to like Dan Green."

I very much liked Dan Green. "Somewhat."

"I think he turns you on." He flashed that dimple. "Okay, I'll walk in behind you. Kendal is staying here, or she hooked up with someone here. You said uniform. Zippo's or NBC. Those are the most likely places she could grab a uniform—I doubt she whipped it together—or stole it. It's a good time to check, before she comes back." Which was why he'd driven like a bat out of hell. "You can say you're here to see the facility. Say that you want to make a donation."

I stepped back. "*Lie?* I'm not sure—"

"Just ask them to see the back. Tell them whatever you want. You need three hundred top hats or something."

"Well...I...do need a tux." At the very least, I could get measured. Maybe try one on. That would ease the shame of missing work. This *was* Poppy's fault after all.

I looked dubiously at the silver lamé draping the storefront and wondered if they even had a black tux for rent. My money was on something colorful and theatrical—something retro with spats. Or spots.

"Tux." Dan's smile softened. "That's a good idea." He took his sunglasses off, tucked them into the placket of his shirt, and his dark-chocolate gaze rested on my mouth. For the first time all day, he focused on my lips, licking his own, and my stomach flipped over the right way. "I can't wait to see you in black tie. Gold cuff links. The whole shebang. Shiny shoes. Bow tie. Jesus. Do you have any silk boxers? We should get you some. Let me get you some."

He moved closer and his index finger stroked my neck. The heat of the sidewalk was forgotten. Smog? Sweat? Carsick? Huh? Dan's finger circled lazily on my skin, and I was lost. His voice grew unreasonably husky. "What will they say, Ce, when we dance together? I want to do that. I want to hold you in my arms, in front of the entire damn world. Would you do that? Would you dance with me?"

Enthralled, I could only nod like an idiot, but the thought—he was just so beautifully comfortable with us.

His lips brushed my ear. "Just the two of us? I'd like that. I'd like it a lot."

"Yeah. Me too, actually."

"You'll let me lead?"

I swallowed. "Maybe."

"Always." He grinned, and his hand cupped my neck for just a moment. He winked and his dimple was so deep I wanted to fall inside his smile and never find my way out. He just...unhinged some locked door inside me...and then he stepped back and checked his fucking watch. "So, make this thing at Zippo's count. Give me enough time to poke around and see if Kendal's shacking up there. Easy breezy."

"Lemon squeezie," I croaked, desperate to stop my dick from hardening anymore while I stood like a lovesick puppy on the sidewalk. I cleared my throat. "Let me just give a heads up to Poppy."

"Sure thing." Dan waited while I texted my best friend—again—to say I'd be late. *Don't lift anything. That's what Andre is for*, I added.

"The sooner I finish this job for Gunter, the sooner I'm free of Shep's apartment and we can take the bike to Staten Island. Maybe I'll be finished by Saturday. The awards are going to be difficult."

I considered that for a moment. "Of course I'll help you, but if I screw this up, I don't want to hear any complaining."

"Deal." He grinned but his eyes were on the street. "I need you to be the memorable one. That's all. You should have no problem with that."

I chose the high road, and this time, I kept my mouth shut.

Entering Zippo's was like opening a portal straight to backstage, 42nd Street. Shiny and fanciful and sleazy. Strands of shimmery silver stars hung on invisible threads from the ceiling. To my right a manikin in full stormtrooper regalia greeted me; to my left a man-sized faux fur chipmunk scared the piss out of me.

The store brimmed with stuffed wire racks and plastic bins. Accessories were everywhere. The aisles bustled with people, something I hadn't expected because the street was fairly quiet. Most of the customers and what staff I could see were women. A chunky sales clerk sat behind the counter. Next to her computer was a stack of catalogues and a pile of slim three-ring binders.

Dan disappeared behind a stand of wigs to investigate, and I swallowed, ignored the hulking chipmunk and went to speak with the forty-something-ish clerk. She wore a tape measure around her neck tied in a half-Windsor and chewed on the end of a pencil. She looked like she was filing invoices.

I needed a minute to prepare myself, so I flipped through one of the binders. It was stuffed with an unusual selection of animal costumes. Panda bears, penguins, squirrels, wolves, teddy bears—they were very well crafted and oddly adult sized. I flipped further until I came across the fluffy visage of an extraordinarily well-endowed red-tailed fox. He smiled slyly back at me.

Holy shit.

I slapped the cover shut. *Disgusting.*

Also, shockingly impressive. I looked guiltily around the store before checking the label on the binder.

Furries.

*Okaaaay.* The binder hit the glass countertop with a crack as I searched for some hand sanitizer.

"Can I help you find something specific?" the clerk asked. Her gaze landed squarely on the binder.

"I'm…I…" She thought I was here for an anatomically

correct fox costume. I cleared my throat. "Do you have any tuxedos?"

"Seriously? We have hundreds." She couldn't be more disinterested. "Through that door. Monica will measure you if you like, but you're a 38 Regular."

"Good eye" was all I could think to say. "Uhm. Should I select a style or something first?" I looked at the stack of binders on the counter.

"It's all on the racks. You can't miss 'em." She waved a paper at me. "Here's the map. Take what you need. If it's more than you can carry, get a rack. You check out here. Monica'll itemize 'em and if you have a car or whatever, the loading dock door is two stories tall. You can't miss that either."

"Loading dock?" I glanced at the map. I'd bought Groucho Marx glasses here once three years ago, but that was as far as I'd gotten inside Zippo's. The furry selection must be new.

"We ship nationwide. You want it? We got it."

"Oh. I just need a tux." I took one last look at the chipmunk, wondering if some conventioneer in Houston had worn it recently to hump a lion, then I headed for the back.

Dan had done his ninja thing—he was nowhere and everywhere. Maybe he was scaling the walls with suction cups on his fingers, searching for clues.

The warehouse itself was vast, dry and thick with dust. Daylight shoved its way through grime-coated windows. It was warm. Very warm. Actually, the place felt like a tinderbox. I passed seven fire extinguishers, and that was in the first two rows. I didn't know whether to be alarmed or relieved.

Giant, slow-turning fans circulated the dirt on the floor in tiny, ankle-high dust devils. Dirt clung to my ankles.

I walked around to scope it out. There was a lot to see.

Clothing of every style, texture and hue hung, some with tubs of accessories below, some on the sort of revolving racks my uncle Vito had in his dry-cleaning stores, though few of the clothes here were covered in plastic. Were they clean? Who did that?

I promised myself that I wouldn't balk over a less than perfectly clean suit.

I avoided the other customers. It had to be a full-time job for ten people to maintain a single section of the warehouse. Costumes were draped, hung, folded, piled and arranged, ready to be borrowed. Frills and gewgaws, feathers and tidbits. The racks were high—sometimes two or even three stories. A woman walked by with an armload of lacy parasols, and I knew that this was one place Kendal could easily hide. It was huge, she knew the layout, and...she must still have friends working here. She had her pick of costumes to hide in—and that's what she had to be doing on the street. Hiding in plain sight. She could be anything, even a dancing tube of lipstick, and who would care to notice her in New York?

Dan suspected this as well or why would we be here? Although, as far as I could tell, Kendal wasn't here right now, so I followed the plan. Such as it was.

I consulted the map. Second level: contemporary menswear. Bingo.

The Zippo's second level of hell was a loft whose railing was decorated with nude dressmakers dummies. They looked disturbingly like headless men. Naturally, a rickety metal staircase led to the *collection.* My turn in the art world informed me that perhaps this collection wasn't a major draw. They should rotate that stock through.

A slim woman in khaki shorts and a sweaty Zippo's T-shirt approached me. She was my age but wore a high-school-girl ponytail. Auburn tendrils poked from her hairline. She looked tuckered from the heat and washed out. Too washed out for her twenties. Her smile was sincere. "I'm Monica. Can I help you find something?"

"I need formal wear."

"No problem." She pointed to the glorified ladder. "Thirty-eight regular, halfway down the third rack. There should be a blue one—"

"Black. Tell me you have black."

"White, green, orange, and if you're lucky, maybe there's a few plaid brown ones. Oh and mustard."

Mustard? "I'm impressed that you know this from memory."

She cocked her head and gave me a patient look. "My parents own this place. I've been here since I was eleven."

I made the family business nice-nice with her. "My pop owns Rocco's. I worked the register too."

"In Brooklyn? I saw that place in the *Times*. They have great cannoli."

"They do."

Her expression changed. She was trying to place me. "You still work there?"

"No. My brother does."

"Hey. I know you." A sunny smile lit her face and she was suddenly young and pretty. "You're the guy from the paper today! The Beemer Basher. Where's your mustache?"

I had completely forgotten. For an hour, my infamy had slipped my mind. How did Shep and Gunter stand being the center of drama all the time? Public drama, I mean.

It was tough, but I raised my lips in something that felt like a smile. "That's...uh...that's my...cousin."

"Oh. You look exactly like him. You could be twins."

"So I understand. Uhm. Since I'm here, I'm wondering if you know Kendal Schmidt? She used to work here." Oh why not? Dan was doing the same thing and there was no sign of him. What was he doing? He should be the one asking questions.

Which meant he must already know the answers.

Monica said, "Kendal? You're not really involved with those actors are you? Like the paper said?"

"No. I'm a caterer. I just wondered if you'd seen her recently."

She didn't bat an eye. Or twitch a muscle. She was remarkably still. Cautious. "Kendal and I worked together. She quit last spring, before graduation. She weaseled a job from Gunter and bye-bye Kendal. She hit the big time. She's really proud now. *La dee. I work for someone famous.*"

"Do you know him? Gunter? He's a piece of work."

Monica hung clothing on the rack beside us, neatening the row, straightening collars and moving a few pieces around to her satisfaction. She checked buttons and plucked loose threads. She was very deft with everything. I realized she was a seamstress. She had those bone-knuckled, long fingers that women who sew have. Strong muscular hands with blunt nails. "We deliver to the studio—I met him once or twice. He's a piece of something, all right. He never asked *me* to work for him."

"She met someone who did. His agent. Right place, right time."

Monica shrugged. "That's how she is."

"Did you know she disappeared?"

"I wouldn't worry about Kendal. She's sly. Like a fox."

My mind's eye instantly conjured the photo of that well-hung fox, and I smiled weakly. "So I hear. You haven't seen her this week?"

The girl glanced around. She tipped her pale face, like she was weighing something, and finally she said, "I saw Lester. Her boyfriend. He was outside when I locked up the past two nights, and again this morning when I opened."

"He was here this morning?" That man really got around. And Monica worked long hours.

She nodded. "Seven thirty. His hand was broken or something. I told him if I saw him again, I was going to report him. He's kind of a creep."

"Sounds it."

Monica moved to help a woman carry a burlap horse head, and I made my sticky, sweaty way to the rickety stairs.

It was good to know that everyone in New York was leery of Lester—was Kendal? Interesting. She was four foot eleven and looked like a pixie. She slept on silk sheets in a harem tent—a sensual experience that had to be lost on Stew, but perhaps I was being unfair. Maybe she was hiding from her ex-boyfriend—a boyfriend who lied to her and, from what I could figure, was bisexual and foolhardy.

I reckoned Jean Luc Pappineau, Shep's dominant and uninhibited lover, would know how to show Lester a good time.

On the second floor, I had a bird's-eye view of the storage facility. It was total chaos. The overstuffed aisles were alive with customers scurrying like mice in a maze, but the loft was deserted.

The rack of tuxedos held all the broken promises I suspected, although the price for rental was temptingly affordable. Twenty-five bucks. As I feared, the suits weren't up to my standard of cleanliness, but I had family who could see to that at cost.

I picked through the rack. Brown. Shit brown. The aforementioned mustard. Blue. Blue velvet. Orange. I ask you. *Orange.* I nearly took it—just because it was orange and I couldn't believe it.

I stopped myself. *Dan.* What he'd said to me on the street. It echoed inside my mind.

*Would you dance with me?*

Dan Albright wanted to dance with me, on a dance floor, in a public venue that had nothing to do with pride parades—and everything in the world to do with pride—and I was going to dance with him and look spectacular doing so or go broke trying.

I flipped to the 40 R's. With any luck, something would fit or I could eat a lot of cake before Saturday.

More of the same brown—they all matched. Probably pieces from a show or movie wardrobe—hello *Guys and Dolls!*—and then, sweet Jesus. *There.* Nestled between a green plaid nightmare from the twisted mind of some Jersey City community theatre costume designer and a flaming gold lamé disco suit was a solid black tux with a single button and a lovely satin shawl collar. I extracted it from the rack like I was uncovering the Holy Grail. It might as well be, because this garment was a miracle. It had saddle stitching. Inside, a hand-stitched label read 38 Regular and the name *Armani.*

I nearly clutched it to my chest. Some angelic Italian hand had sewn this, and someone else had misplaced it. Not within the rack. No. This was a treasure and should, by all rights, be on another city block, in another store. Something with *Threads* on the sign. Something in Soho—and it should have a nine-hundred-dollar price tag.

Twenty-five bucks! Joey would eat his blue tuxedo over this score. I smoothed the lapel. There was a dressing area around here somewhere...which turned out to be a curtained-off square down an ill-lit hallway. It was tucked right beside a row of deserted offices.

I was minding my own damn business, just me and my gift from God, when I pulled back the curtain and Dan snatched me by the shirtfront. "Hey. There you are."

He yanked me inside and—*fucking-ay*—I yelped like a kicked puppy.

"*Jesus. Shit. Fuck. Shit.*"

White light danced behind my eyeballs. I flung his hand from my shirt and blinked back pain. Something felt—torn. It hurt to breathe. Correction. I couldn't breathe. It wasn't due to the adrenaline blast—which FYI wasn't doing me any favors here—it was because my stupid injured ribs burned like a band of flaming painful fucking *pain* around my chest.

"What's wrong?"

I gasped. "Goddamn it, Albright, you cocksucker. Knock it the fuck off."

Dan stood goggle-eyed in front of me and I didn't care. "Sorry," he said. "I didn't mean to scare you."

"Didn't you? You have to stop doing that."

"Hey, I'm serious. I'm sorry. Really." He smoothed my hair back from my forehead. His hair was still neat, though a little sweaty now—he'd have been a pod person otherwise—and dust flaked his shirt.

I wheezed, "What are you doing here?"

"Checking the offices." He nodded down the hall. "I heard something and I stepped in here." He looked contrite for a split second, and then understanding brought a stern note to his voice. "Forget all this garbage. Let me see your chest. You never showed me."

"I'm good. It's just a bruise." I was feeling better already. I must have been bent the wrong way.

Dan was peeling my shirt away. "No. You whine, but that's just for fun."

*Whine?* I knocked his hand away. "Quit it."

"Why? We're behind a curtain. This is a dressing room. Where else should we do it?"

He exposed my stomach, inching my shirt higher.

I gripped his wrist. "Listen to me. We're not having sex in here. *Capisce*?"

He stilled—and then he had the nerve to laugh. "What are you talking about? You have one dirty mind. And a devious one—you're hiding something. You're hurt. Lift your fucking shirt, Romano."

"No. I'm fine. The seat belt bruised me. 'Tis only a flesh wound."

He didn't laugh. He yanked my shirt to my armpits while I tried to wrestle it down.

We both hissed at the explosion of color staining my rib cage. It was slightly worse than this morning.

Maybe more than slightly.

"Jesus Christ, you idiot. Did you tape this yourself?"

"I don't like your tone. I followed the instructions on Google, but like many things one uses the internet for, I could only use one hand."

"You're not funny. Just hold still." He stripped one line of tape away and while it stung, I refused to whine. He had no problem bitching. "You did a piss-poor job."

"Hey, I tried. It was hard."

"That's what he said."

I laughed and—ow. "Don't make me laugh yet."

Dan coaxed the last piece of tape away and tossed it in the dressing room trash can. His fingertips stroked the healthy skin above my bruise. "Your ribs are bruised, you frail little shit."

"I am not frail. And no kidding—I can see it." It was a mean purple and black. Very *Fight Club*. "It didn't look like this earlier."

"You should have said something."

"It's not that bad, so stop freaking out. You just jerked me wrong."

He raised a brow.

"It's not like I ruptured my spleen." I hoped. I frowned a little, because I couldn't remember where exactly my spleen was housed.

"I'm still not thrilled." Dan's shoulders brushed me and just like that, he was in my space, taking my air. His hand skated around to hold my spine, palm hot on my back, and his eyelids grew heavy. "While we're in here, why don't you let me kiss it and make it better?"

That liar had done it again. He wanted to have sex here.

I opened my mouth to say something sarcastic, but he silenced me with his tongue. He licked that delicate line inside my lips, tasting my teeth, and as he delved in to stroke the center of my mouth, an intense, dazzling rush of pleasure weakened my resolve. After such an insanely shitty day, the sweet promise of Dan's lips made me cave instantly.

The Armani fell from my fingers. It was somewhere with the fallen pins and discarded hangers on the dusty floor. I'd go to hell for that alone, but I hooked an arm around Dan's thick neck and sealed him to me with a moan. His mouth wiped every thought from my mind. He eased every ache—except the one rising inside my pants.

His palm soothed me from mid back all the way down to my belt line, until he held my ass in his hand. We stood there lost to the warehouse, our tongues dancing, dipping, sliding, every noise dissolving into the white hum of need. Squeezed together—his steamy chest was flush against my bruised one. His lips moved, supple and skilled.

I rimmed his mouth. Sweet. So sweet. Lips like sugar. I held his jaw and tasted him again.

He stopped long enough to ask, "Seriously. You're good, Ce?"

"Yeah. I'm good. I'm good." I drew him back to me, reeling him in with a kiss and a small nip on his whiskered chin. I think at any other time, in any other place, we would have turned desperate—we had a history of setting the sheets, walls, floors, even the shower on fire. This time, we held back. It wasn't my injury—I'd been wobbling around all day—it was more. Something had changed. His kiss was tender. Mine was earnest. He cradled me, and I pet his shoulder, until we were simply holding each other. Kissing chastely in the dressing room like gentlemen.

The sound of shoppers filtered through the curtain, and the whir of the industrial fan still blew dust along the floor, but inside the ugly room it was safe and private. We were an eternity away from Zippo's. Transported to our own secret hideaway.

Even his smell—cardamom, cigarettes, mint and sweat—held a new note. And fuck me if it wasn't the piney, magical scent of Christmas trees.

Ribs be damned, I slid my hand into Dan's pants and let my palm meet the engorged shaft of his penis. He moaned, "Oh yeah," and I curled my fingers around his thick stem. His kisses landed between his words. "We don't have to... You're hurt... This can wait."

"Just undo your pants, Albright."

Dan swallowed, but he did it—he worked his belt quickly and his cock was suddenly free and happy and home in my hand. He tried to say something and I cut him off. "You're not actually going to turn me down, are you?"

He pushed into my palm, his dark eyes looked straight into mine. "Never."

I went down on my knees on that filthy floor. I was careful not to touch anything dirty except Dan Albright. The heady combination of man and savory shower gel filled my head as I soothed his angry erection with a kiss. I ran my tongue from the top to the bottom, and Dan's palm came to rest gently on the back of my neck. No force or grip, just assurance.

I suckled the velvet tip, his hips flexed forward, and I guided him inside the warmth and comfort of my mouth. I held his hips—as much to steady myself as to keep from touching the dressing room floor.

Downstairs the clacking of a loading door rang through the building, and I froze and looked up to meet Dan's steady gaze. He breathed, "Jesus, baby. I never know...what you're going to do next...but please don't stop now. Nobody knows we're here."

A curtain divided us from a warehouse full of women. It was broad daylight. He just...did something to me. Brought out the kink in me.

It took only minutes—a flying passage of time—until Dan's other fingers curled around my nape, seeking purchase somewhere, and he pumped with smooth strokes inside me. "Suck me, Ce. Harder."

His fingers pulled the ends of my hair, digging into my scalp for that single second when rhythm and speed got confused and he couldn't seem to find either. I had him covered. I fucked his cock with my sucking mouth and brought him to orgasm. It was fast. Salty, sticky come burst deliciously inside my throat, and I swallowed without letting go.

He shuddered above me until I eased him, kissing that spot at his thigh where his leg dipped into his groin. His hair tickled my nose.

Dan helped me to my feet. Before I could ruin this incredible moment with a glib or stupid remark—because now I was both nervous and exposed—he kissed me until I forgot what I was going to say.

He kissed me until I was breathing heavy, forgetful of my bruise, and I reached to grasp his biceps, digging into them with my fingers. His chest rumbled. The bastard was laughing at me with his pants down around his thighs.

"What's so funny?"

He nibbled my ear. "Nothing. Everything. You. Me. Us. I have to go get that twit Heidelbach and take him to his next appointment."

"I could make you stay, you know." Ever alluring, that's me.

"No doubt about it." He kissed me again and then he retrieved the fallen Armani—such a sacrilege—from the floor, and I dusted it. He said, "This room has sexcapade written all over it."

"We can always come back again."

"We could. Right now, you need painkillers and a hot lunch, and I have money to earn and a fool to protect."

"Rain check?"

"Agreed." He mothered me one last time, looking at my ribs, muttering "Jesus fucking Christ" under his breath.

I figured if nothing else now was as good a time as any to try the tuxedo jacket on.

It was infinitely improved once it was on me. *Damn.* Like it had been made for me alone. Heavenly. There was no question I had gotten lucky. I was keeping this thing.

Dan checked me out, and then he swallowed hard, his Adam's apple working with a click. He ran a calloused palm over my satin lapel with care. The rasp of his skin was nothing like his voice. "This one's a keeper."

# Chapter Ten: Lies and Misdemeanors

I breezed through the door of Posh Nosh at 2:15 in the afternoon holding a garment bag over my shoulder. I was five and a quarter hours late for work and my uncles were waiting for me, the two of them hunched over cups of piping-hot black coffee at the Formica lunch counter. They had my red velvet cupcakes. I didn't bother to ask if those were the last two.

"Caesar. Where you been?" My uncle Vito's voice bounced through the small shop. I wouldn't kiss his ring or anything ethnically stereotypical like that—why bother?—but I let him hug me. I hid a wince as he put the squeeze on my tender spot.

I smiled and said, "Out." That was standard speak for none-of-your-business.

My uncles look like every other blood-related Romano in Brooklyn, except that Vito shopped in the Big and Tall department. He was built like a rectangle. Not fat, but he was a solid block between his shoulders and knees. I had not inherited the Romano height, and he had missed out on the speedy metabolism. He should have saved that cupcake for me. I was so disappointed. I sighed and consoled myself with a chocolate chip macadamia nut cookie.

Vito nodded. "What's with the hat?"

"That stupid thing in the paper." I hung the Armani carefully on the coat rack.

"Everybody is calling. Phone rang all morning. I ripped it outta the wall," Tino grumbled. "I don't wanna talk about the paper. I'm liable to lose my temper."

"You and me three." I shook Tino's hand and tossed the hat.

There were a few patrons sitting at the small, scattered tables. Most of them had sandwiches and lovely, pricy cold salads. Everyone had a dessert, of course. I cheerfully calculated they'd spent about nineteen dollars apiece. Thursday at two, the place was quiet. I'd arrived in time to do little except prepare for Shep's party. My tardiness may have worked to my benefit.

"That your boyfriend?" Vito squinted at someone on the sidewalk. He nodded using only his chin. "Outside there? Who's that man he's with? He ain't seeing someone on the sly, is he?"

"What? No, of course not. He's not even here. He's—" Dan and Jorge Carrera were across the street. Jorge Carrera. My stalker had one foot casually on the stoop—Mr. Savoir-Faire—and his camera and bad hair decision were with him. It would be a service to all of mankind if he lost them both.

Carrera gazed blandly at Dan, who was puffed up like a rooster. He looked imposing. Threatening. Obviously he was setting some ground rules for the intrepid reporter. I should handle this myself, but Dan might be questioning that sneaky bastard. Besides, I was finally at work. I should stay put. "Dan just dropped me off. Honestly, I thought he was gone. He has a big thing."

Vito blinked at me.

"A work thing."

"He's a cop. They're always working. Always skulking.

Always on your tail." While this was true, especially of Dan who liked my tail very much, I didn't dare throw any fuel onto Vito's anti-law enforcement fire. His expression was based on years of cultivated dislike. "What's he doing anyway?"

"Looks like he's scaring that asshole reporter off—"

"Reporter?" Vito stood so fast the seat of his stool spun. "Is that the reporter who wrote that garbage about you in the paper today? You looked like a Guido in that picture."

Tino stood too.

"I am a Guido." I grabbed a Perrier from the beverage case and stuffed a slice of lime into the top. "It's fine." It wasn't fine, but I wasn't in the mood to be an accessory to murder. Not that my uncles would actually murder anyone, but they might know someone who knew someone who could. "Let Dan handle this. He knows the law; he knows my rights. I trust him. So you need to trust him too."

Vito sat down. "If you say so, but I'm not too sure."

"I am. So look. About tomorrow night, swear to me you won't scare Shep or any of his pretentious friends. Be polite. Be professional. Don't make any sudden moves. No fake accents. *Capisce*? Shep likes you both and tomorrow night is important." For Poppy—this had nothing to do with Shep, really. I hoped we'd score a few new wealthy clients.

"What? Whatdaya mean? Scare people?" Tino chuckled and elbowed his brother. "How'd we get such a reputation?"

"I cannot possibly imagine." Why had I hired these two? They were going to be a handful. "*Listen.* Please. Just act normal for two flipping hours. Here's what I need you to do—"

The door to the kitchen swung open and Poppy wobbled in holding a flat delivery box. She beamed. Every Romano rushed to assist her with her burden. It was in our blood. Scolding her didn't work, but I tried anyway. "Put that box down. You promised."

"Don't be a dink. It's a dress box. I can carry a dress. Move." She butted me out of her way with her hip and set the package on the counter. She was vibrating with excitement. "It just arrived! Joey had them deliver it."

"You had your Soapie's dress delivered here?"

"I wanted to...show you," she said a little self-consciously, which was no way for Poppy to say anything. "I'm nervous. I'm thinking my baby bump will diminish the heat level of this dress. It's going to make me plain cute instead of scandalous and borderline slutty."

"You always look gorgeous. Stop digging."

Vito swallowed uncomfortably. "That boy needs to marry you before I'm a grandfather. I don't want nobody calling my grandkid names. Especially not by other people's names, if you hear me. What are you worried about sexy? You're expecting. You're practically married."

"What century do you come from? This is New York. I'm not dead yet. I'll marry Joey when I marry him and not a second before. I'm not walking down the aisle with a maternity panel sewn in my gown. That's just not on my to-do list." She turned to me. "You just don't say anything."

"Who me?"

Tino ate it all up. "You're a good girl. Of course you'll be beautiful in that dress. It's not red, is it?"

The doorbell jingled and Dan entered with a blast of warm air. He had my messenger bag dangling from one hand, and his sunglasses perched on his head. He looked more like a dashing pilot than a private eye.

I smiled and took a bite of my cookie. He smiled back.

Vito's smile dissolved. "Hey if it ain't the cop."

Dan didn't slow. "Don't you have some money to launder?"

Poppy choked on a laugh and stage whispered to me, "Ce. He is such a keeper. And *muy caliente.*"

I took my bag from Dan and, *zing*, that unhappy puppy sound escaped me again. I tried to cover with a cough, but that hurt even more and it became apparent that I was now...*yelping*, for lack of a better word. I felt like such a pantywaist. With the tape gone, my ribs were bothering me, especially if I moved the wrong way. Which now bordered on every way I moved.

I held onto the counter until my coughing-trying-not-to-cough spell passed.

Dan took my bag back and settled it on the counter. "If you're not better by tomorrow morning, we're going to the walk-in. Nod yes."

"I—"

"I don't care what else is going on—or who we're supposed to be working for—this comes first."

"I—"

"And don't tell me again you're fine. You keep making that face—and you're clutching your side, Romano."

I dropped my hand. "I'm fine."

Tino and Poppy wore identical expressions—sort of slack-jawed at Dan's newfound fussiness and concerned over the strange noises I'd made. "I'm fine," I said to everyone.

Tino said, "What's a-matter with him?"

I wasn't sure if he meant me or my bossy boyfriend, but between Dan's intrusion with Carrera, the scene in the dressing room, and this—I was sort of unnerved.

"Nothing. Nothing is the matter with me." I shot my *please shut up* look at Dan and he countered with a stony *you take care of yourself or I'll really make a scene* glare. I said to the benefit of everyone in the listening audience, "I'm a little stiff from the...collision yesterday. That's all. I just need a couple Motrin."

"Well it's a good thing you have some right here in your bag. I'll wait while you take them," Dan said. "Have four."

"Four? You're turning into a control freak." But he was absolutely right, so I did it. Poppy disappeared into the ladies' room with a Bergdorf Goodman garment bag while Vito closed in. He moved one shiny stool over and entered Dan's personal bubble.

Dan's shoulders stiffened.

Vito leveled his steely gaze on my tense boyfriend. My uncle was frighteningly direct. "You know what? I want to know something, Albright. I want to know what's the story with you. Rocco and Ellie called me this morning. They say you haven't taken my nephew upstate to meet your fancy family. What's that all about, 'cause that ain't right in my book. You two are—what do you gays call it? An item. And for how long? Couple months? We do things differently in our family."

I refrained from pointing out that neither I, nor anyone in our entire extended clan, had a clue about Poppy and Joey until she had skipped a few periods.

"Isn't he good enough to meet your folks? Why do you keep blowing him off?"

"What the hell are you talking about? We're going this weekend." Dan's confusion was plain.

"Caesar said it got cancelled again. He said something came up—this is the fourth time. Fourth. People who cancel that many times? They don't want to do something. They make excuses and weasel out. What's the matter with you?"

*Mia famiglia.* Dear God. "You people gossip too much. I've

met Dan's aunt. Get your facts straight."

"That's different. That was work." Vito swatted his square palm at me like I was a gnat. "Stay out of this. Nothing wrong with people talking to each other. I think he's afraid to commit. Look at him. He's upset."

I said through my teeth, "I would be upset too if his family put me on the spot like this. Do you mind? This is none of your business. We're going on Sunday. I misspoke last night."

Now Dan turned his puzzled eyes on me. "Misspoke?"

I swallowed. "I just thought that because of the Soapies, and everything, we'd take another rain check. No big deal. I told my mother I was cancelling until...a better time. My parents are...intense. I'm sorry." I heard "Here comes the bride" from some dark recess of my subconscious mind, and I reached for the Perrier.

Honestly, my mouth felt a little dry.

Dan honed in on me as he slipped into his detective role—quickly abandoning his hovering, sexy, protective-boyfriend mode. I didn't like being on this side of his scrutiny. He said, in a voice so flat you could cook a pancake on it, "You've cancelled three times. If you don't want to do this Caesar, say so. I don't want to force anything."

Everyone stopped. Or maybe everyone receded. I stared at Dan who stared wordlessly back at me as he waited with perfect calm.

"I..." Why didn't I want to go to Westchester? What was I so fucking afraid of? They weren't vampires, they were just people.

What if...they didn't like me? Or worse, oh man, what if I didn't like them?

What if...

Poppy flounced through the restroom door sparkling like a

fairy princess. She was breathtaking in cherry-red beaded chiffon. It hugged her slender frame and plunged in every direction. She was gamine and graceful, and I latched onto the vision of her like a drowning man clings to a life raft when his ship has already gone down. Poppy tossed her impossibly blonde hair and smiled. “How do I look, fellahs?”

But Tino shushed her. “Quiet. Quiet.”

Her face fell a little.

“Yes or no,” Dan said. “I can call them. It’s not a big deal.” Dan was lying. I saw it clearly. It was obviously a very big deal, and now he didn’t want me to know because I’d blindsided him. He was hurt. His voice didn’t pitch or waver, and he wasn’t joking or flippant. He wasn’t hiding or acting. He looked sharp and ready to tackle the next problem.

Which, for the moment, was me. I was the next problem.

My heart pumped shame into my face. I was *such* a crappy boyfriend.

Dan waited for an answer so I mumbled a weak, “Yes...of course...I do. We’ll go. I’m just...just a little nervous. You haven’t actually...told me anything...about them. That’s all. That’s it. I’m...just...I...I...I...”

Zingo. My affliction nailed me.

Poppy gasped.

Vito and Tino wore matching round-eyed expressions.

And Dan’s nod was as sharp as his jaw.

“Right,” he said and checked his watch. “Time to go. I gotta get uptown. Gunter has a shoot in twenty minutes and I need to bring the car back.” His teeth tapped together as he spoke. “You stay clear of Carrera, and call me if you see anyone. I’m serious about the ribs.” He pecked my cheek, and then the door jingled. Dan was gone in a flash. He’d practically run.

"Shit."

Poppy smacked my arm and I winced because it flipping hurt, but not as bad as the pain tearing a hole inside my chest.

"What the hell is the matter with you? Oh my God, Caesar. You lied to his face. That poor guy. He's totally in love with you."

*Love?* "No he isn't. He likes me. He's pissed that I...I... And I'm not the only one with commitment issues, Poppy McNamara." I glared at where her thickening waist should be thicker. "What did it take for you to commit? *Oh wait.* That's right. You still haven't."

"Low blow, dickhead."

"Is it? You should marry Joey. You love him. He loves you. You're a family. Marry the guy. But I'm just not...ready to...go to Westchester and...be...be..."

"You love him. You've already committed, you fucking dumbass." She flounced into the public restroom and slammed the door.

Not long after that edifying exchange with Poppy, I swallowed two Vicodin—probably ill-advised (Nana handed them to me with a refreshing glass of orange juice—she wasn't licensed to practice medicine, but she was a veteran Dr. Mom) and I took to my bed. According to Google, I was nearly at the kick-off stage to the real pain. According to Caesar, airbags were the devil's handiwork.

It was going to be a while before I could sleep on my right side, but I had a left side, so I wasn't going to complain. Since the warehouse sexcapade, my skin had turned an appetizing aubergine. I spent my evening cuddling a bag of ice, and then I drugged myself into oblivion and crawled between my soft cotton sheets. The thread count was hardly Kendal Schmidt quality, but it was home just the same.

I pushed Bella to the end of the bed with both feet and stared groggily at my phone charging on the bedside table. I should text him. I should, but I was too stupidly proud to make the first move. It seemed weak, even though I was in the wrong. He probably needed a little space and I knew I did. Maybe he'd call me when he was ready; maybe he'd never call again.

Clearly we'd entered a new stage in our relationship, something deeper than sexcapades, dinner and a movie, and yanking each other's tail. We'd advanced to the meeting-each-other's-parents and hurting-each-other's-feelings stage.

And the fact was I needed to apologize for lying. Not for my cold feet—I was entitled to cold feet—I wasn't ready to meet Mr. and Mrs. Albright of the Baxter-Miller Albrights of Westchester County. His uncle was Riley Albright the senator. It felt like pressure.

I wiggled, and finally abandoned my dream of finding a comfortable position. I was uncomfortable from the skin in. I'd just lie in my lonely bed of fear and regret and trace patterns on my ceiling. How pathetic...

I woke on my stomach, cheek stuck to the pillow with drool as some sixth sense yanked me from my Vicodin slumber. There was a sound in the night. Something out of place. I strained to hear above the dull hum of the air-conditioning—but it was quiet. No noise now except Bella, deep asleep, purring and pinning the back of my knees to the mattress.

I heard it again. A creak coming from somewhere downstairs. That was no figment of my pharmaceutically enhanced dreams. Maybe it was the kitchen door. Maybe the window. Whichever, I concentrated on the sound emanating from the back of the house as the skin on my neck crawled.

There was someone in the house.

On the nightstand my phone glowed 3:24, meaning Nana wasn't downstairs looking for a drink of warm milk—or bourbon-laced tea. She didn't wander, not this late, and if she had gotten up, she'd flip the hall light on.

A scraping noise filtered through the floorboards. It was subtle, but it was followed by the unmistakable clatter of a kitchen chair as it hit the linoleum. Whoever was here, they stumbled clod-like in the dark over unseen obstacles.

My pulse kicked into overdrive, rattling the bruised cage that protected my heart, and my head cleared. I forced myself from the covers despite the pain. Not kidding. Google doesn't lie. I was lucky it didn't hurt to breathe.

A foot landed with poorly executed stealth on the hallway floor. The heel of a rubber shoe squeaked on the wood. Sneaker was my guess. A man simply because statistics told me so.

A man in sneakers was currently prowling in the dark, tripping over our furniture because he wasn't familiar with the layout, and he was heading toward the stairs.

Screw this. Caesar Anthony Romano didn't take intruders lying down. He met challenges head-on, unless they were matters of the heart, and then he hid from them beneath the covers.

I slid from the bed, listening with such strained effort the entire house seemed to vibrate around me. Outside, the street was about as still as it ever was—slow cars, the sound of planes above, the bark of a dog. If this turned out to be my thirsty grandmother in rubber-soled bedroom slippers, I didn't want another embarrassing mention in the paper. But Nana came first. She was a seventy-six-year-old widow and I was her only protection.

I didn't want to give my position away, so I texted the only person I could. *Call 911 intruder in house*—shit I hoped he woke up—then I went for my weapon.

In the corner rested the Louisville Slugger my father had given to me when I first moved in with Nana. I'm not a noted sports enthusiast—go figure—but this bat from my pop was the Romano equivalent of a housewarming gift.

I gripped it in my right fist, exactly as I'd been taught, and waited in the doorway wearing only a pair of white Hugo Boss underwear. They glowed pale blue in the night. Shit, way to make myself a target. I should shuck them, but meeting an intruder in the nude seemed more than a little rash.

I steadied my aim, and the air around me crackled with expectation. My room was at the top of the stairs, so if this was a simple break-in, they could have the toaster and anything else we kept downstairs. But if anyone came up here—and the only reason to do so would be to harm one of us—I'd bash his brains in.

Footsteps crept the length of the hall beneath me. The purple shadows seemed dense with menace, every shape an intruder or a villain. The bathroom doorway was a darkened portal, the bottom of the stairs an inky well with no movement below.

Why the fuck didn't we ever leave a light on? My grandfather's penny-pinching CPA reign had ended years ago. For fuck's sake, we could pay a dollar more a month to leave a damn nightlight on.

The first footfall hit the bottom stair.

Instead of fear, anger flooded my veins. Swinging a bat into some thug's head, it was a little like venting my spleen. I stared grimly into the hallway and Bella, that whale, growled low from a foot behind me.

I almost dropped the bat on my foot. "Sss-ss." I hissed at her to go away.

The intruder froze on the second, maybe third step. We all halted in our tracks. I was about to flip the light and do something athletic with the bat, when Bella channeled a charging rhino and tore down the hall, all thirty-five pounds of her. She spat and howled and scared the bejesus out of whoever was on the stairs.

I slapped at the wall to find the seldom-used light switch as the patter of running feet fled down the kitchen hall. I flung myself after him and almost tripped over Bella's fat ass as she wailed on the landing. I barely caught myself on the banister.

That cat nearly killed me.

The door swung as our intruder disappeared through the kitchen. Jesus. I finally let loose with a robust, "*Get the fuck out of my house!*"

"Caesar! Who's there? Oh my God! What's wrong? Are you all right?" Nana arrived at the top of the stairs, clutching her nightgown to her neck.

"Go to your room. Lock the door and call the police."

In the kitchen, the curtain fluttered—he was gone.

I wasn't about to hurl myself through the fucking window into a dark alley, alone, in my underwear, so I bolted for the front door. Hitting the locks and flipping the chain, I raced outside, careening to a halt in a pool of yellow street light. The sidewalk and street were empty.

It was hot as blazes. The neighbor's dog barked from the alley. Parked cars waited ghostlike for morning. A delivery truck shifted gears two blocks away—otherwise it was still and peaceful. Across the river, the city lights made a rosy hue against the overcast sky.

Whoever had broken in was gone, leaving me gasping for air with a lung that wasn't too interested in cooperating.

"Caesar." Nan was backlit in the doorway. She held my bathrobe. "You're in the street in your underwear. Come inside." She didn't mention the bat. She knew what it was for. I swung it onto my shoulder, pretending that move didn't hurt and that it was manly to hyperventilate, and I went into the house.

"You were supposed to go upstairs."

"What's wrong?"

"Nothing." I took nice easy breaths and slid into my robe. My phone vibrated. "I'll lock up, Nan. Go wait for the police. Please. I need to know you're safe."

Her face was pale with anxiety, and for the first time ever my nana Cooper looked old.

"It's okay." I patted her arm and kissed her forehead. "He's gone."

She nodded, still clutching her gown. "Thank you, pumpkin."

I answered the phone on the way to the kitchen, flipping every light in the house as I walked. It was Dan. I kept my voice even. "Sorry to wake you."

"What's going on? What the hell's wrong?" His voice was thick. "I got your message—patrol car should be first to arrive."

"We had a break-in."

"You're all right, then? Did you see anyone?"

"No, but I think Lester Finch just dove through the back window." In the kitchen where I'd had ravioli with my nan only hours earlier, the charming café curtain was askew and a chair was on the floor. "He somehow managed to jiggle the lock."

Which was odd, since at least one hand was splinted.

"What? Are you sure—?"

"And before you ask me, *yes*. I'm sure. Whoever it was stumbled through the house like an amateur, tripping over the furniture and running away when the cat meowed. After yesterday? It just makes sense that it's Finch."

"I was going to ask you if you're positive he's gone. Did you secure the house?"

"Oh. Yes. He shot out of here and disappeared as soon as Bella attacked. You told me not to worry." My forehead felt impossibly tight, and I pinched the flesh between my eyes with two fingers. "Shit. He could have hurt my grandmother. What if I hadn't been here?"

Dan was firm. "But you were there."

"What if I wasn't? You said I was safe."

"I had no reason to think otherwise. You're overwrought—do you think I would put you at risk if I thought you were in danger? You or Nan?"

"Of course not."

"You're staying with me until this is over." We fell into silence, and I sensed he was as overwrought as I was. He confirmed that with a shaky breath. "Jesus Christ, Caesar, you nearly killed me with that text. Do you need me to come out there? I will. None of this matters. Nothing else matters."

"No. No, you need to work. I'm okay, I'm just...we'll go to Pop's."

He cleared his throat. "That's a good idea."

"I'm sorry," I said stiffly. "For...waking you."

"Don't be an idiot. It was a solid move. If you hadn't texted—then you would have to apologize. You're sure you're okay?"

"Yeah. Thanks." The front hall window flashed with blue light as a patrol car arrived. "I can't talk. I need to deal with the police." I was too edgy to talk anyway. "But Bella scared that freak away. I've never seen her run for anything but a can of tuna before, but she chased that asshole from the house. She's a hero."

"So are you, baby. Lock the doors. I'll see you in the morning—keep me posted. Take care of Nan. And take some Motrin."

# Chapter Eleven: Straight Up

By seven Nana and Bella were settled safely with my parents. I put my father in charge of the locks, a pet interest of his held over from the days of his misspent youth with Vito and Tino, and somehow I managed to catch my train into the city. A busy, busy day lay ahead of me before the shindig at Chez Gay. I needed to bully the florist, I had to run uptown to do a final look-see, and I needed to pester my uncle for a better deal on the booze. He expected as much and would be hurt if I didn't at least put in the effort to get everything at cost.

It was a mystery to me how Poppy ever managed without my help.

With an arsenal of painkillers and fresh catering duds in my gym bag, I rode the clogged subway train into Manhattan with a thousand other commuters. Sweat trickled under my armpits and loosened my binding. It was going to be another brutally hot day in the city. The air was charged with electricity and thick with ozone—perhaps someone had been fried on the third rail—but it felt like a long overdue storm was on the way. Right now the sky was clear and blue, but pee-colored clouds hung ominously along the horizon. Maybe that was just New Jersey.

My phone rang as the subway jostled along. "Hey, Mom."

"Caesar."

"How's it going?" She wasn't one to call this soon after a visit. Mother and daughter under the same roof must be causing some strain.

"Nana rearranged my new living room suite and invited me to yoga because, and I quote here, *your thighs look a little loose.*"

I snorted. Poor Mom. It was rare, but it happened—Nana was bored. "Send her to the senior center. Tell her they need help updating their virus definitions."

"Maybe. But I thought you should know that your license is here."

"My what?" *What?* "Here where?"

"At the house. Did you know that if you find a lost license and drop it in a mailbox, it shows up at the address listed? I did not."

"You're making that up."

"I am not. It came this morning in the mail. I'm holding it in my hand and I cry every time I see your photo—you have to swear to me you'll never do that again."

"Believe me, I promise."

"I have it here whenever you stop by."

The train stopped. Hm. I hadn't even noticed we were approaching my stop. I fought my way out of the car and climbed the cement steps to meet the wall of humidity on the street. I wouldn't think about last night—I'd let the police handle it since they were better equipped to do so—but I kept a sharp eye out for anything unusual.

Because this is New York, I was having a hard time differentiating between usual and unusual. Still. My eye was honed.

I resurfaced on West 4th Street, blue sky, sun shining its golden rays of morning on the city, and there—exactly like yesterday—smack in front of me, was Kendal Schmidt. She was in the bloody crosswalk again, and I froze solid, not exactly the smoothest move ever, but I was convinced she was a hallucination. Maybe this was the aftereffect of Vicodin?

No. That was definitely Kendal hot-stepping her miniature fanny through the crosswalk, her blazing ponytail bouncing along behind her. More unbelievably, she was dressed in the same cop uniform as yesterday. You'd think a seamstress of her caliber would exercise some creativity. She had that entire warehouse at her disposal. She could be anything.

I tugged my cap low, put on my sunglasses and hit the sidewalk, set to follow her. Uncanny that she was here on 4th just as I arrived for work. Her apartment and Zippo's were a quick walk away, sure, but so was Posh Nosh.

I slowed, letting pedestrians cut by me, and checked my watch. 8:55. Same time I came to work every single day. Like clockwork I arrived either by the F train or Dan's bike.

Kendal's fiery hair swung jauntily as she skipped onto the curb like a schoolgirl and disappeared around the corner.

What the hell was she doing *here*?

I had the good sense to hang back. It was crazy thinking, but what if she was looking for *me*? Not that she would be, but...hypothetically speaking, she could be. I'd been in the paper—my name sandwiched between Gunter Heidelbach, *Puppy Lover*, and Sheppard McNamara, *Actor*—and I'd been at the dealership with her ex-boyfriend whose fingers I'd broken. Twice. I'd gone into her home on Waverly Place and fondled her sinfully expensive bedsheets. And that was before I recognized her on the street. I'd spoken with her neighbor, and then fellated my boyfriend in her former place of employment.

My God. That woman knew who I was.

I think.

What if Kendal wanted to find me specifically? Hell, if anyone wanted to find me, my personal life was splayed all over the Internet thanks to the ex-boyfriend I had mistakenly started to like as a person again—Sheppard McNamara, *Publicity Whore.*

My job, my photo and my home address—Google owned me. I mean, that didn't make me any more special than anyone else on the planet, but I had been careful all these years. I had been circumspect and lived a clean life, discounting all the sex in public places I'd enjoyed recently with Dan.

I baked under the radiant morning sunshine, and rational thinking leaped out the proverbial window. My rash thinking climbed inside to take a quick, impulsive look around, and I whacked that bastard down with a firm hand and called Dan. "Where are you?"

"Hello to you too. I've been roasting in this fucking car all night." I took that to mean he was on a stakeout. "Where are you?"

He was understandably cranky if he was in the Camry, so I dialed my tone down. "I'm two blocks from work. I can't even believe I'm saying this, but I just saw her again."

"Saw who again?" Dan was chewing on something. He was a former cop, so ten to one he was eating a donut.

"Kendal."

There was a pause—a pause that might have been Dan scrambling to pick his breakfast up off the floor. "How do you do it, Ce? Seriously."

"Do what? I just got off the train. That's all. I'm on my way to work."

He sighed. “I’m starting to think I should pitch all the law-enforcement training and follow you 24/7. I’d have better luck.”

“Maybe you should. Maybe I should be the detective and you should be the caterer.”

“Why does that sound dirty?”

“I wouldn’t know,” I said primly, although we both knew I intended it to be dirty. I felt like we were back on equal footing. “So, obviously Kendal’s home base is down here.”

“I know. I’m on it. Just don’t do anything.”

“What exactly would I do?” Other than follow her—*which I was not going to do.*

“Oh, I’m positive you’ll think of something. Just hang tight. I’ve got it covered.”

“If you think I’m going to do something rash, you’re mistaken.” I dismissed my absurd idea that Kendal was interested in me. This mess with Kendal and Lester and Gunter? It had nothing to do with me. I was only a lowly caterer and Dan, Mr. Law Enforcement Training, didn’t need any of my *untrained* assistance—although I’d found Kendal twice and he hadn’t laid eyes on her, to my knowledge, a single time. Not that I was keeping score. “I’m not about to be late for work again. We have a gig. And you’re bartending.”

“Jesus. Don’t remind me,” Dan muttered, and he disconnected.

*Fine.*

I pointed my feet directly toward Posh Nosh—do not pass go, do not collect two hundred dollars—and Jorge Carrera, sporting a chic gray fedora and Tom Ford sunglasses, rose from the underground. Oh, for crying out loud. I had done absolutely nothing, and here was another one of Dan’s people of interest.

Jorge hitched his expensive camera bag over his shoulder.

His stringy hair must be coiled under that fetching hat. He did look very East Village today, so I gave him points for trying.

I ducked into the green grocer until the paparazzo disappeared around the corner. He was following Kendal—the woman he showed interest in from the start—or he was headed to Posh Nosh to pester me in some newfound way. What was his deal? I simply didn't understand his fascination with me. Granted, I was Shep's first lover, but that was old news. It was evident that Jorge was following someone.

I was in the act of texting and walking-while-dodging-pedestrians (the one sport I'm good at) when I glanced across the street, and as soon as Jorge rounded the corner, Lester Finch emerged from the busy Starbuck's.

I dropped my cell, jerking to catch the slippery son of a bitch, but tenderness in my upper extremities made it impossible and my precious phone flipped from my fingertips. It smacked the concrete—*crack*—and the screen shattered. Another hundred bucks—gone. Unsurprisingly, the battery separated and bounced into the storm drain.

I was officially tired of this entire week. Thank God it was Friday.

I jumped as spritely as I could manage, given my trussing, back into the doorway of the green grocer. With all my stop and go and hopping around, I'm sure somewhere someone in the Village was reporting my behavior as suspicious, but that was too bad because I'd bagged all three of Dan's most wanted in four minutes—without even trying.

Maybe I *was* in the wrong line of work.

Lester's eyes were hidden behind a pair of Terminator shades. They were vaguely threatening and a little childish. His hands sported matching finger splints. The hulking blond didn't have a hat—and for him, that disguise would have actually worked. In one bandaged hand he held an iced Venti. It had a straw and a mountain of chocolate-drizzled whipped cream. His splints stuck out like blades from around the cup as he sucked greedily on his beverage. Lester waited on the corner for the light to change and smiled at an orange-haired waif beside him.

I kept from sight until he made it safely to the opposite corner. He then headed west.

Where were these people going? And what bad guy drinks a Frappuccino during a chase scene? And did I have enough time to pop in and get one? I'd skipped breakfast.

I retrieved my ruined cell phone from the sidewalk and crept forward enough to look around the corner. Lester's hatless head bobbed cheerfully away from me in the crowd. He was as carefree as a kid at summer camp. Drinking his drink. Enjoying the morning. Waving at pretty girls with his silvery splints.

How could this happy idiot be the same criminal who broke into our home and terrified my elderly grandmother? He breezed along without a care in the world, *tra la la*, with his "I love my mother" tattoo and his six-dollar iced beverage.

I glared at the back of his knuckled head, now half a block ahead of me, and I found myself...following him, which was an act of rashness expressly forbidden me by a certain bossy PI, but I didn't want to lose sight of Lester and I couldn't reach Dan.

As frighteningly distasteful as he appeared to me, and as odd as our interactions had been, I couldn't find a single reason for Lester Finch to terrorize me specifically. Other than the fingers—but even that, why would a man with no police record commit a felony over what was essentially a misunderstanding? It was too extreme a step—and too risky. He had absolutely nothing to gain from breaking into my house.

I made it as far as the corner, one short block from Posh

Nosh, when the light changed. I pressed the button on the crosswalk and glanced to the left. Dan's white Camry was parked in a line of cars on the side street. Lester was now a block ahead, having crossed moments ago and theoretically, since Dan was on a fucking stakeout, he should be on that. He had peeped; it was time for him to lurk. Wasn't that what the car was for? To follow suspects? But oddly, it didn't budge.

Why was he just sitting there?

I could go tap on the window and say hello, maybe scare him for all those times he'd yanked me into a closet, alley or dressing room, but I wouldn't blow his cover. This was the real world and stakes were theoretically high.

I waited for the light to turn green and the Camry's passenger door opened. Jorge Carrera climbed out. I peered over my sunglasses just to make certain. His obnoxious camera was in his hand as he said one last thing into the car, he cupped the lens in his palm like a giant phallus, and nodding, he shut the door. He didn't come my way to pursue Kendal—the newsworthy, noteworthy, newspapery choice—he headed in the other direction. Which just so happened to be toward Posh Nosh.

The Camry was next to move. I could practically smell it from here—or maybe I smelled a rat. Dan slid the car easily into traffic, and the urge to hurl my broken phone at the windshield was almost too much to quell. He drove nonchalantly past me, one square, scarred hand on the wheel, his elbow sticking from the driver's window. He was chewing gum as he merged into traffic and headed in the same direction as Finch and Schmidt.

The light changed and I stepped into the crosswalk, listing and discarding possible reasons for Dan to meet with the reporter. He was either covering all his bases because he was worried about my safety after last night, or he was pissed that I was a magnet for his suspects and wanted Jorge to report on my whereabouts. It could be both. Or neither. How smart of him to choose Carrera since he had a hard-on for me anyway. I'd never suspect the dogged photographer. I'd just think the guy was a prick.

I thought the guy was a prick anyway.

I headed toward Zippo's—or as I'd begun to think of it, *Kendal's Lair*—and enjoyed the reasonably fresh air and the bright sunshine. It was a nice day. Small birds hopped along the sidewalk looking for French fries, and middle-aged mothers chatted on cell phones and pushed fat toddlers in high-end strollers.

There was another explanation for Dan speaking with Carrera. Diversion. If Carrera was on me instead of whatever truth Dan was protecting, aka the *big story*—as Gunter said—then it would be imperative to keep the pain-in-the-ass reporter occupied elsewhere.

It took only a few minutes to arrive at Zippo's. I circled to the car-choked alley and used the exit beside the massive loading-dock door. There was no way I was using the front door. I slipped inside Zippo's Costume Emporium at exactly nine fifteen in the morning and pocketed my glasses.

The warehouse was the same as yesterday. A jumble of fire-code violations surrounded me, but I used the squalor to my advantage. I hid next to a towering stack of discounted fabric, my gym bag slung behind me. Dusty, hot and dry—wool and cotton fibers floated in the air and filled my nose. The ceiling fan swirled. Between the fabric rolls, the multiple stories of hanging clothing and the weak light, I couldn't see a damn thing. I didn't have a phone to call anyone—Dan, the police or Poppy to say that I'd be running a few minutes late today, so I eased along the wall, working my way to the loft. There I'd have a bird's-eye view of the enormous facility, and I could find a phone in one of the offices. I grabbed a handful of parasols to hide behind and hastened along, pretending to do something costume-centric and non-threatening. I'm sure not a soul noticed me as I climbed the wobbly stairs to the loft.

There were plenty of women bustling below me, searching the racks and pushing empty carts to start their shopping, but the second level was as quiet as it had been the day before. I went straight to the office to use the phone and before I moved five steps in that direction, goddamn his eyes, Dan popped up like a gopher, slapped his rough hand over my mouth and dragged me into the racks by the strap of my bag.

He hissed, "So much for staying out of trouble, Romano. If you weren't already hurt, I'd wring your fucking neck."

I wrestled his hand off. "What are you doing in here?"

"What do you think I'm doing here? This is my job. I'm working. I would ask the same of you, but it's obvious that your idea of *not doing anything rash* and mine are two different things. You dope."

I was too embarrassed to speak, but I did so anyway. "I just...I thought...my phone died..." I redirected. "I have a question. Is Jorge following me?"

"Of course he is. Be quiet and stay low. Kendal is in one of the offices." He kept his gaze on some target below us, but now that we were stuffed in a stiflingly hot clothing rack, I was too short to see. Dan grumbled, "How're your ribs?"

"Tender. I may have over medicated. You could have given me a tiny heads up about Jorge. And I can't believe Finch—"

"Ssssh." I thought he wanted me to stop bitching, but no, he drew me further into the musty darkness. "He's coming."

"Who?"

"Finch."

Lester Finch's heavy feet clomped on the rickety stairs and the loft shook. He cruised past our hiding place with a poufy opaque garment bag flung over one massive shoulder. He'd lost the Frappuccino and he'd gained a tiny blue cell phone.

Dan's breath was on my ear. "Be still."

I nodded, mesmerized by the vision of Lester's fingers wiggling like tentacles as he held the phone. His voice was brimming with joy. "I'm almost there. I can't wait to see you too."

He pounded purposefully across the loft. It struck me again that Lester behaved as if he had nothing to hide. Every one of us was hiding from something or someone, some of us less cleverly than others (case in point, Dan and I crammed in our nest of seersucker) but Lester was visible and eager to reunite with Kendal. If the smile on his face were any indication, he didn't care who saw him. He acted innocent.

Or he was just a moron.

He disappeared down the empty hallway.

"Should we...do something? What if he hurts her?"

"I don't think that's an issue. I'll check."

"I wonder what he has in the bag."

"I don't think you want to know." Dan nodded toward the stairs. "Hey, why don't you go on? I'll meet you back at Posh Nosh in a while. You can buy me a cup of coffee and a slice of that chocolate ganache cake. I'll text you if I run into any trouble." As if that ladle of bullshit wasn't enough, his smile was a dead giveaway. I wanted to pinch his cheek and tell him how cute he was.

"What are you hiding?"

All innocence, Dan answered with his typical non-answer,

"What? Why would you think—?"

*Clang clang clang clang. Clang clang clang.* The fire alarm nearly ruptured my eardrum, and I jumped, smacking Dan's jaw with my forehead. His teeth clacked together against my face. "Ow. What the hell?"

I hoped to God it wasn't a real fire because then we were all doomed. I looked around for the exit sign as Dan tugged my sleeve. "C'mon. Fire door is this way."

We cut through the clothing and cruised by the dressing room where our last sexcapade had occurred only yesterday. "I still can't believe we did that."

"Believe it." Dan led the way down the hall toward the emergency exit. *Do Not Open. Alarm Will Sound.* What a shocker that the door was ajar.

"Well that explains—" Dan halted in his tracks and said in disgust, "You have got to be kidding."

I looked around. It was just an ugly hallway with no décor and three doorways, not enough to stop and offer commentary in the middle of a fire drill.

Then I saw Lester.

"Holy crap." On the mud-colored carpet of the third office, Finch lay splayed on his back. He twitched and blinked at the ceiling, his mouth slackened. He was oblivious to me and Dan watching from the hall. I was gaping. Dan's mouth was pressed together in a rigid line making his morning whiskers stand at attention on his chin. He sucked his teeth in resignation and then he hauled me into the dingy room by my elbow and shut the door with his foot. It was a tight squeeze in the room. Really it was only big enough for a desk and a chair. "Of all the stupid..."

Dan bent to check Lester's pulse. "He is the biggest dork ever, isn't he?"

The fire alarm cut off as suddenly as it started, and we were treated to the sound of Lester Finch moaning.

"Well, I'm not one to judge, but yes, I think so. What's wrong with him?" I couldn't grasp what I was seeing. Lester was in some sort of twilight state. And something else was odd. He had changed his pants—these were made of two-tone brown…fur. He had on fur pants. Maybe he was in a play? "Is he having a seizure? Should we do something? What happened?"

Dan didn't appear concerned in the least—but he was experienced in emergency situations so his blasé attitude meant nothing. "Kendal lured him here and tazed him." He dialed 9-1-1 on his cell and I waited as he gave the dispatcher the information she needed. "Stun gun. My guess is she fried him while his pants were down."

"Stun gun?"

"I've seen them in a few stalking cases. Women prefer tasers because they fit in a purse and they level the playing field without causing lasting damage."

"It certainly leveled Lester." He took up most of the floor with his twitching limbs. "Shouldn't he be coming around by now?"

"To get a guy this big down, she hit him more than once. Safe to say she was sending him a message."

"Message received. Maybe I should get one for Nan."

"Not unless you want her to go to jail. They're illegal in New York."

Lester was still down, but occasionally he'd mutter or grunt. How ironic that he'd been felled by such a mouse of a girl. Given Lester's choice of trousers, I wondered if that was the literal case. "What's he wearing?"

"Remember that boss of yours who got off on having sex in clown shoes? Some people like to dress as animals." Dan nodded. "Meet Lester Finch."

"He's a *furry*? I saw that catalog downstairs. I never dreamed that..." My eyes bugged out. "Gun called him an animal on purpose, didn't he? That little pissant. He knows this? You need to tell me right now if Gun is into this furry thing. Right now. Not that there's anything wrong with it—" I remembered Gun's PSA with the puppies and I felt queasy. "I'm sorry to be a prude, but this is plain weird."

"It takes all kinds, and no, thank God, Gunter's not into this." Dan looked tired—he had lavender bruises under his eyes from lack of sleep. His clothes were rumpled, and today he smelled more like air freshener and stale coffee than bad chicken. "Gunter's got enough problems because he's tied to Kendal. It's worse than you think."

"I can think some pretty bad things." I looked pointedly at Lester who flopped against the leg of the desk as he tried ineffectually to pull himself to sitting. He made slow grabs at the air. His splints were reminiscent of wolverine. That had probably titillated him until Kendal fried his ass. "How worse?"

With one foot, Dan pressed Lester gently back onto the rug. "Hold up there, buddy. You need to wait a minute."

Our dazed and furry friend settled.

"How worse?"

One of the things I most respect about Dan is his ability to cut to the chase when he chooses to. He did it now. He leaned against the wall, crossed his arms and looked me straight in the eyes. "I'm not going to lie to you when you ask me a direct question, even when it's about my job, you know that. Sometimes I have to keep things...but I'm not going to lie to you."

"It's our version of Don't Ask Don't Tell."

He smiled. "I'm in this for the long haul, Caesar. I want you in my life." My eyebrows rose proportionately to my jaw unhinging. "This is confidential, you understand? I'm breaking a professional confidence."

"I...I don't know what to say, except that you don't have to do that for me."

"Yes I do. We're at that point."

Talk about straightforward. Touched, I reached and stroked his hand. "I want that. Too. For us to be together. I'm sorry I was such a dick yesterday. Really."

"You weren't a dick. You were afraid. We're in no rush—my parents can wait. I thought you *wanted* to meet them—that you were expecting it. I thought it would make you happy."

"Me? Uh. No." I added hastily, "It's not that I don't want to meet them. I'm just not ready to meet them. I'm...you're right. I'm scared shitless."

"I can relate. I'd rather you meet my grandparents."

"No. I'm scared shitless...of this."

He nodded. "I know. But you don't have to be."

Lester smacked his lips, and the moment between Dan and I dissolved.

"So, okay. Tell me your secret. I'm braced for something upsetting."

"Good, because they were sleeping together."

"Lester? Forget what I said. That's *disgusting.*" The man was drooling on the carpet wearing plushie legs. "No way. Gunter Heidelbach was *not* fucking a chipmunk. He despises Lester."

"No. Not Lester. Listen to me carefully, Caesar. Gunter was involved with Kendal. They were having an affair."

"No. That's not possible. She's a girl. And he's on our team. That man's flame burns brighter than mine. He's gay."

"Not really."

"What do you mean, *not really*? Like not all the time? What is he bi, like Jean Luc? I can sort of see it, but..." I shook my head. "I can't see it."

"No," Dan said with finality. "Not. Really."

"What? But..."

Dan nodded and I stared in confusion until some closed door inside my mind creaked opened.

The first time we met, in Shep's breakfast room, what had Gun said to me about the newly out actor? *He's shoplifting my niche.* And Dan had called Gun a *real* Casanova. I remembered the German ogling Poppy in the front hall, and I couldn't shake my head hard enough to clear it. If Gun was swinging both ways, Poppy needed to stay far away from that good-looking, grabby-handed German. "What?"

I was about as coherent as Lester Finch as the facts arranged themselves and only truth remained.

Dan waited for me to catch up. He leaned his head against the wall and stared at the bare ceiling. His voice was gentle but firm. "Believe me, I know how you feel. It was a shocker for me too, but he's straight. It was Estelle's idea. He's flamboyant no matter how you look at him, so he didn't have to broadcast his sexuality to the press, like Shep—who played straight for how long? Everyone assumed Gun was gay. There was no announcement or press conference. Gunter and Estelle didn't correct anyone. He's been a closeted heterosexual since he was twenty-two."

"That's just total bullshit." My shock skipped denial and swooped straight to anger.

"Nope. It's true."

"Why would anyone go along with that?"

"Bad representation. Bad judgment. Naiveté. Youth. Take your pick of reasons."

"Those aren't reasons, they're excuses. Gay men pretend to be straight because they have to, not the other way around." But he'd done it so believably, never once had I doubted his sincerity or...Jesus...his *authenticity*. "That's the stupidest, most shortsighted stunt I've ever heard of."

"No question about it, and he's paying the price now."

"This is outrageous." I was gearing to get militant, but for fuck's sake, we were on Christopher Street, the very birthplace of the gay rights movement, and Gun's betrayal hit me right where it counted: in my pride. It was hard enough for anyone to find the courage to come out, never mind be proud, and Gun had played our identity for fame. Which was so strange and ironic, I actually had to sit down in the battered office chair. I was sick. My knees felt weak. No wonder Gun was terrified of Kendal. "That idiot is going to be the poster child for every asshole who thinks the rest of us can be straight if we only try a little harder."

"Yup. He knows, which is precisely why he's kept quiet."

"Bullshit. He's kept silent because of the scandal."

"That too. He played along—thoughtless? Yes. He was young and he made a terrible mistake and he trusted the wrong people. Believe me, he's paid for it. You'll see."

Sirens sounded from the street below us—an emergency vehicle, fire, ambulance or police. It didn't matter to Lester snoring blissfully at our feet. The freak had fallen asleep.

"Gun should come clean." My God. I wasn't really militant, but I was a stickler for honest living. I'd said those very words to Shep for ten years. Gunter's hand snaking across the settee replayed in my mind. "Oh my God. I told you he made a pass at me. You're sure he's not bi? Just a little bit? I could see that."

"Maybe. Hey, if I were straight, I would make more than a pass at you." He winked, and then he got to it. He stood and dragged me along with him. "But it doesn't matter. He can't have a scandal before the awards ceremony. Afterwards? Who knows. Right now, I have a job to do and so do you."

"All right, Albright, I won't say anything."

"Good. This is his story to tell and he wants to do it on his own terms."

"No one would believe her anyway. She could say whatever the hell she wants—she could post photos of him fellating Alvin here and no one will believe he's anything but Gunter Heidelbach, *Actor.* I can scarcely believe it."

"Took me about five minutes. Once I saw the truth, I couldn't see otherwise. You'll see."

"Stop saying that. And by the way, you lied to me." I punched him in the shoulder.

"Yup." He shook his head sadly. "You're never going to keep this secret. The sooner I'm done building this case against Kendal, the sooner he's safe."

"I get it. Jesus, how am I going to be able...to...to...to...say he's gay if...he..."

"That's the beauty of his lie and why he's lasted this long. No one is ever going to ask."

# Chapter Twelve: Door Prize

By some miracle I pulled the van into the alley at four o'clock, right on time for the party. It was a sweat-draining ninety-seven degrees. Traffic clogged every street and choking exhaust thickened the air. Thunder rumbled over the distant swamps of New Jersey and the clouds rolled on the horizon—the sky was darkening. Before this evening was over, it was going to piss rain.

My ribs ached, but that wasn't due to any fluctuations in the barometric pressure. I'd reached my limit of over-the-counter painkillers, and now I'd have to suck it up for the rest of the evening.

I climbed stiffly from the van, and Jorge Carrera entered the mouth of the alley with his camera in hand. Man, he was quick. So quick, I wondered if he'd hitched a ride uptown on our back bumper. You had to give the man credit for his persistence.

Jorge was on me in a flash. "Caesar. Just a sec. What do you know about Gunter's former secretary, Kendal Schmidt?"

"Nothing more since the last dozen times you asked, Jorge." He'd buzzed around me like a busy bee all freaking day, his ponytail trailing behind him like a limp stinger. Every time I stepped from the kitchen at Nosh, *buzz buzz* Jorge-bee. Every time I walked through the side door. Every time I went to the bathroom. Every time I answered the phone. I had my own personal paparazzi and he was unrelenting, but it bought Dan and Gunter the time they needed. With Lester's statement, they had enough evidence for Gunter to file his petition. Kendal was officially a stalker and the police needed to speak with her—and good luck to them finding her.

I unlocked the back of the van—and my chest seized again. "*Fuck*."

"You okay?"

"Sure. Fine. Look, if you see this girl—since you're so interested in her—maybe you should introduce me."

"Is she coming to tonight's party? What kind of party is it? Are there costumes involved?"

"Costumes?" I smiled. "Now what makes you think there's even a party tonight?"

Jorge stared at the catering van. "Uhm..."

Uncle Tino climbed from the passenger seat dressed for tonight's festivities in traditional waiter garb—black pants, white button-down, gold chains. He threw the back door open and proceeded to load a case of booze onto the dolly. "You don't lift nothin', you hear me? I see you do anything strenuous and I'm calling your mother." He jerked his thumb at Jorge. "Who the fuck is this? He botherin' you?"

"No, not really. He's the reporter who wrote that article about me the other day. He's the one who called me a *secretary*."

Tino's shrewd eyes narrowed on the reporter. My uncle flexed his knuckles, and Jorge smiled weakly and said, "That was just a misunderstanding. I'm so sorry. I'll try to catch you later, Caesar." He scrammed to join the host of reporters mingling on the front steps.

"Thanks."

"Forgetaboutit. That was fun, but don't tell your aunt. Not your mother either."

At Shep's door, Dan's friend John greeted us by checking a plastic clipboard to see if we were "On the list." Unfortunately we were, so we entered the foyer wheeling a dolly of booze.

"Some place." Tino whistled. "That Shep did all right for being such an a-hole."

Stephen flitted into the entry and looked worriedly from his iPhone to my uncle. The fetching young twink sported a pink and black polka dot pocket square and tie. "Mr. Romano. Your...er...uncle is waiting in the kitchen. If you need anything, don't hesitate to ask."

I was surprised he remembered my name, but with his phone in hand, I realized he was using it as a kind of cheat sheet. "Fine. Tell Shep we're here."

He shot another nervous look to Tino and then Stephen disappeared into the study.

I'd been in the kitchen for a minute when the door swung inward and Gunter arrived in a cloud of gorgeous sandalwood aftershave. His chin was baby smooth, his dirty blond hair was slicked behind his ears and his robe was open to his knees. "*Liebling*, I haff heard that you ah injured."

I looked for telltale signs of his straightness, which was politically incorrect of me, I know, but honestly? The man deserved an Academy Award. "I'm fine, thank you for asking."

"You ah fine indeed." Gunter's eyes gleamed. I couldn't tell if he knew that I knew, but he must. His gaze lingered on my mouth for far longer than was seemly and, as one does under such circumstances, I licked my lips. He winked.

"Knock it off, Gun."

"You take away all my fun, but still I like you."

Man, he was good—and damn it, I smiled reluctantly back at him. "I like you too, but when this is over, you and I are going to have ourselves a little pow wow. Tonight you keep your hands where I can see them."

"I will haff an announcement soon enough."

"I may know a good reporter for you. He's looking for a big story and he's pathologically committed to finding it."

"They are parasites."

"Yes, but sometimes it's good to have the right person on your side."

"I would rather have the right person behind me. Will you assist me?" Gun's lascivious wink was ruined when he lifted the cover on a platter of stuffed cucumber cups. He made a face.

"Uhm. Thanks, no. Maybe you could cinch the robe? I can see your razor stubble."

He cinched his robe with a sad look. "I am to be your host. Shep is sequestered in his room preparing himself."

I could only imagine. "So, it went well today?"

"We have filed the papers and now we wait for the police." He added a sincere, "Thank you, Caesar."

"*Prego.*"

Someone coughed and I turned to find my uncles wearing matching expressions. They were curious—eyeing Gunter with great interest, sure, but Gunter had mentioned the P word.

"Police?" Vito grunted.

"It's a...uh...formality."

"This one of them TV personalities you were talking about?"

"Gunter Heidelbach, meet Tino and Vito Romano, my

uncles from Carroll Gardens."

"It is a pleasure to meet the family of such a desirable man."

Before Gun dared to bat those mile-long lashes at me again, I said, "Okay. Out. Time to work. Go find your pants."

"I will leaf you to work, but I am not looking forward to sharing host duties with Shep. Perhaps later, you will find time to keep me company?"

"Perhaps."

"Your friend, Poppet? She is coming?" His brows lifted. "She will haff to do."

I should have rented a burka while I was at Zippo's. Whether Poppy was committed, sort of, to my cousin or not—it would be hard for anyone, man or woman, to resist Gunter's star power. Joey was going to kill me if I let Gunter maul her. "Have I mentioned my uncle Vito is her soon-to-be father-in-law?"

Gunter shook Vito's hand again and clapped him on the back. "Congratulations. I think she's a delicious little tart."

Oh my God. "Yes. Be that as it may, we have work to do. If you'll excuse us?"

"Ah. I will go smoke my final cigarette."

"It's a party, not a firing squad. Try to have some fun. You're perfectly safe here."

We went to work. My uncles handled the bar, as uncles do, and got loose in the living room. I went to the kitchen to liberate a foie gras Oscar statuette from its mold.

Sometime after five, Stephen popped through the swinging door as I was scouring Gunter's shaving sink. It only took a single pubic hair to bring a catering company to its knees, and since we were already on our knees, Heidelbach could accidentally slay us.

"Mr. Romano?"

All three Romano men turned to the crisp young assistant and said, "Yes?"

Actually Vito grunted, and Tino said, "What?"

Stephen cleared his throat and announced grandly, as if he were a butler instead of an assistant, "Mr. Albright would like a word."

"Tell him to come in here. I'm working."

"He said you'd say that." Stephen flourished a piece of paper from his pocket and handed it to me.

It was a Post-it note. In Dan's firm script one word was written—*Please.* I carefully refolded and pocketed the Post-it. As love notes went, it wasn't much. I wiped my hands on a linen towel, folded my manly apron and went to get dressed.

In that very same back bedroom where Dan and I first crossed the line from acquaintances to lovers six weeks ago, my pressed pants and shirt lay waiting on the enormous four-poster bed. Dan was stretched comfortably, resting against a stack of pillows. He was eighty percent dressed in a white fitted dress shirt with the collar open and a pink Posh Nosh tie hanging untied around his neck. He had the obligatory black trousers and black socks. His shoulders looked three feet wide in that shirt and his waist was slender. He was damn hot for forty.

His legs were crossed at the ankle and when I came in, his fingers stilled on the keyboard. He really needed a haircut, but his damp hair curled at his ears and I liked it. His jaw was about as smooth as it ever got.

"You had your shower?"

"Yup. You came much quicker than I expected."

"You said *please*. How could I resist?" He set the laptop on the bed and I shut the door. "Thirty minutes until show time. I spoke with Gunter and I have to say, it went far better than I expected. No stuttering. You're absolutely sure he's not bi?"

"Sure enough—it's not like I have equipment to measure his straightness, Ce."

He was so terribly wrong there, but I refused to foster his conceit. "Any news?"

"Lester denied breaking into your house and gave a rock-solid alibi. You broke his fingers, you know. Cracked them. He thinks you're trying to hurt him."

"Me?"

"You. And Kendal flew the coop with a thousand dollars worth of Zippo's merchandise. She could be anywhere dressed as anything—Zippo's is checking their inventory, but that will take time."

I remembered Monica. "Her friends will lie for her. You think Kendal will try to come here?"

"I have to assume she will."

"Okay, so how many people do you have watching the place?" I slid my top shirt button free—I needed to be dressed and on the job before Poppy arrived. Dan's gaze flitted briefly to my fingers.

"Tonight? Including John? Five. Every entrance, and there's someone disguised as a guest."

"That sounds expensive."

"It is."

I relaxed enough to loosen the next button as Dan watched. He was sprawled on the bed. His hot gaze followed the flight of my fingers as I unbuttoned my shirt. We had twenty minutes, tops, before we had to be in the kitchen serving the guests. The building was brimming with cops, press and minions like myself, everyone atwitter for the arrival of stars and starlets. My uncles were in the kitchen depleting our stock of sherry, my ex was on the other side of the wall polishing his Ferragamos...and naturally, something—namely lust—came over me.

I wanted him.

Not exactly a newsflash, but right now, I saw him less as my sex-addicted boyfriend, and more as my...partner. I had time all day to think about his admission, and the fact of the matter was—I wanted him for the long haul too. If that meant I had to practice being honest with myself, and with him about what I wanted, so be it. I'd be brave, because I was... I swallowed hard just thinking the words...I was falling in love with Dan Green Albright of the Baxter-Miller Albrights of Westchester County.

That wasn't much of a newsflash either.

Dan crossed his arms lazily behind his head. His chocolate-colored eyes were focused on me like he expected something, and his foot jiggled. "How are your ribs? Should we tape them again? Or are you feeling better?"

I slid a button from its hole and Dan's attention wandered back to my fingers. He stared raptly at my hands as I unfastened my shirt. *Hmm.* "I've surpassed my recommended daily allowance of ibuprofen, if that's what you're asking, but maybe some fresh tape after the shower would help."

"Yeah." He looked up and I knew he hadn't heard a word. I smoothed the placket of my shirt, finding the next button, and Dan's gaze followed again. Clearly, he wanted me to undress for him. His foot jiggling increased as my hands toyed with the button.

He wet his lip with a tiny flick of his tongue, and the bedroom suddenly felt overly warm.

Flick. The buttonhole released its prisoner, and my captivated boyfriend licked his bottom lip again. Strong teeth bit into plump flesh, and his gaze lifted to meet mine. A little thrill shot through my groin.

I moved my hands lower, stroking my chest and nimbly unbuttoning my shirt. Slide, flick. Slide, flick—until I untucked my shirt tails and eased that very last button from its mooring. My hands came to rest on my belt.

Dan's foot ceased moving, and he swallowed thickly in the quiet room.

I ran my thumb over the buckle, fingers cherishing metal, and changed course, moving to unbutton my cuffs. Flick. Flick. I shed my shirt with deliberate care and let it flutter to the carpet. My taped bruise was revealed in its rainbow-colored goodness, but Dan's attention was riveted somewhat lower.

"Hurry up. We only have ten minutes alone until tomorrow night, could you just hop to, baby? Quit fucking around. Take your pants off and come here."

I nearly laughed, but his trousers were tenting and so were mine. "You could always come here and take them off me." I freed my belt and fiddled with my zipper.

"We never fool around in bed anymore." Dan sighed, and he stripped the tie from his neck with a yank. He briefly considered it. "I wish we had time to use this."

My reply was embarrassingly breathy. "Me too."

He flung the tie on the bed and stalked me. His shadowy irises turned so dark they were nearly black. His expression altered from interested bystander to my personal predator.

When he stood inches from my chest, he flattened a hand on the door by my ear. The spicy scent of aftershave surrounded us. His shirt brushed my chest. His lips flirted on mine—and finally, they brushed so softly, I eased against him to get more.

He didn't kiss me. Not quite. "Strip, you little tease. Take your fucking pants off. I'm going to have you right against the door."

"Oh." I bit my lip as his stern words sent another flood of lust straight to my aching crotch. He was so depraved.

Thank God.

"That sounds...incredibly erotic." I struggled to yank my pants over my erection, but Dan's hand took charge and he dragged my pants to my knees.

"Oh, just like that, baby. Right there. Don't move." I couldn't. My legs were trapped. And I swear, my cock could not be stiffer. Its fat pink head reached for Dan. He breathed lewd words in my ear. "Look how much you like that, you dirty thing. I can't wait to get you home. I want to be inside you. I want to slide right inside until I can't go any farther. I want bury my fingers inside you. I want my cock so deep you can't think about anything but me fucking you. You want that too, don't you?"

"I...I..."

His tongue traced my lip and he whispered, "Don't fight it, Caesar. Let go."

I was in his arms, wrapped so tightly my skin chaffed on cotton and wool. Sensitive. Hypersensitive. His belt buckle was cool metal on my stomach. I fingered his fly and Dan's hand circled my wrist. "I don't think so. Not yet."

He pinned my hand to the door, and I squeezed my eyes shut, so overcome with need for him that I wanted to hide.

Dan laced our fingers. His smooth jaw nuzzled my shoulder, and a hot kiss opened on my neck, suckling me hungrily until I broke my silence. "Suck on me."

I needed him. I craved him. He sucked my collarbone, and I humped into him, for the first time ever wanting to fuck him.

My cock found a place inside the hot V of his trouser-clad legs, and I thrust into that tight spot like I was trying to drill him. Pleasure skittered across every nerve ending. I held his neck in one hand, and the other squeezed his fingers as he held me immobile against the door.

"Oh, yeah. Just like that, Ce."

I couldn't get a better stance. My feet and legs were bound, but I ground into his crotch, stumbling over my inane love talk. "Please."

He kissed the corner of my mouth. "Please what?" His erection throbbed thick against my stomach.

"Let go of my wrist. Let me touch you."

I was gliding, sliding, grinding into that prickly, fiery spot between his thighs. His big body held me against the door, just like he said.

"I know your secret now. You want to fuck me, don't you? You'd like that." He gripped the globes of my ass and helped me work myself into a frenzy against him. "When we get home, I'm going to let you."

Oh, God. His words...inside him. Deep inside. "Yeah. Oh yeah."

Teeth met my lips, biting, then his tongue stroked my neck, tasting. He kissed me like he had all the fucking time in the world, and I desperately shoved into that hollow, chaffing my cock on wool and biting back at his shoulder. Cotton filled my mouth, and I wanted to tear a hole in his shirt with my teeth.

"Take my cock out."

I broke, losing my stride and opening my eyes. "What?"

"Take it out."

I fumbled, frantic that my clumsy hands weren't more effective. I was so close to coming that my fingers shook, but at last his trousers were down and he fell into my palm. My breath sawed crazily as I tried to find release. Dan's tongue plunged inside to shut me up. His tongue pushed deep, deeper and he let go of my ass to grip our dicks together. I tipped my throat to swallow his kiss and dug my fingers into the thick of his shoulders. I latched onto him, eyes wide open, and he flung me into a scalding orgasm with his thrashing fist wrapped around both our cocks. His stiff hand worked hot and rough on our flesh. His eyes were dark and wide and I climbed inside his gaze. I let go. I let go and free fell into him. Everything earthly gone except this union between Dan and me.

Shit. I love him.

I had no time for romance because my balls imploded, shoving ejaculate from my body in a blast that soaked my chest and hit his chin and stole my air. I didn't care. I quaked and cried and Dan witnessed it—nothing to hide here. He came too. He came, both of us transfixed by the tough slide of his hand on our joined bodies.

I collapsed against him, desperate for air or space or...Jesus a drink would be a very good thing...and let go of his hair. He hugged me.

"You okay? Was I too rough? Your ribs. I didn't mean to be so—"

"Just give me a second to catch my breath. I'm fine." I was hobbled in my clothing and soaked with come like some kind of perverted boy toy and I laughed. "Oh my God. I must look like..." I didn't want to even think of what I looked like.

"You look pretty good to me." His mouth moved on my neck again. "I love the way you give yourself like that—just for me."

"I have hickeys all over my neck now, don't I?"

"Maybe one or two." Someone banged on the door and Dan slapped his hand over my head to keep it shut. That was ill thought because his hand was slimy. He smiled, the one with the dimple and the waggling brows and then, in a voice that always made my heart swell, he called, "Yeah? Just a fucking minute."

"Could you two have your quickie somewhere else? People are *arriving.* We can hear you," Poppy stage-whispered through the door. She ruined her snit with a giggle. "Oh my God, *guys*, get your fucking rocks off later."

Music, loud, and smatterings of laughter came from the hall. Work. Fuck I was late for work. *Again.*

"Uh. Be right there." To Dan I said, "You need another shirt. Chop chop."

"I'll borrow one from Shep. No worries."

I moved to go, but Dan shook his head. "Not so fast." He kissed me, mindful now of my bruise. We touched lips softly and I held him. Maybe he held me. He was so warm. He smelled like mint and spice and home. And sex, of course. We stayed close until finally I shoved him away with both hands, and with a sheepish smile I said, "You're late for work."

I went into the bathroom to clean up.

# Chapter Thirteen: Party All the Time

The party was surprisingly uneventful—and still no sign of Kendal Schmidt. No mysterious paisley packages were delivered. No eager reporters burst in unannounced. Dan was a respectable, handsome bartender who kept one eye on the door and remained anonymous. Vito and Tino hovered over the far-too-beautiful Poppy McNamara, giving the evil eye to any man who tried to look down her dress.

At first, Poppy fretted over the food and sent messages back to the kitchen via Stephen. I returned a single message that included the f-word and she left me alone. Shep's party wish was to conquer the room—which was his job as the host—so he was hearty and happy and blindingly good-looking. He laughed at everyone's jokes and offered cigars and flashed his big white teeth. Naturally, it was Gun who conquered the bloody room. Everyone loved him, the little faker.

I spent the evening limping in the pristine kitchen, loading trays and removing liquor from my uncles' hands. Eventually, Stephen Taylor popped in to check with me again. "Are you driving back to the Village tonight? I could use a ride."

I was surprised he remembered where he lived—I was also relieved not to drive downtown alone. If I collapsed tonight, and there was a chance I might, someone should be around to scrape me off the sidewalk. "Yeah. No problem. Maybe you could give me a hand unloading the van."

"Absolutely." Stephen flicked a piece of dust from his lapel and said, "Does it involve lifting?"

Truthfully, it wouldn't involve a damn thing. My pain had grown insistent, and like a nagging wife or a crying infant—it wouldn't quit. With each dish I dried, my binding loosened and my deodorant failed. As the party drew near its end, there was no way I could haul myself, never mind wheel a dolly of supplies to Posh Nosh unassisted. The very thought brought a prickling to my eyes—that could be the stale cloud of tobacco smoke that hovered near the ceiling. "Lifting? Not really. You could roll a few racks in for me. I'm a bit stiff tonight. Everything else can wait until tomorrow."

By eight, I was gray with fatigue and, as farfetched as this may sound, I was too tired to whine or fuss (out loud) or even fuck.

Possibly I'd overdone it.

I drank cold Perrier and add another 600 mgs of Motrin to my bloodstream. The FDA would not approve. However, they weren't here to load the dishwasher. I couldn't even eat a fudge macadamia caramel-coated brownie I felt that shitty, so I consoled myself with impure thoughts about the leftover ice from the bar—I wanted to lie with it.

Poppy swung into the kitchen with Gunter on her arm. She was delicious in a miniscule black silk cupcake dress and trendy zippered shoes. A navy blue bow tied under the scooped bodice of her dress. Her beautiful hair curled around her shoulders in some girly, flirty style that suited her, and I was green that she looked as great on Gunter's arm as she did on mine. Still. She sparkled like a diamond of the first water, and as her best friend I tried like hell to sparkle back.

She kissed my cheek. "Thank you so much."

"You're welcome. Just remember this when I need to take a couple days off next week." I needed to go to the walk-in clinic tomorrow before I took to my bed—or Dan's bed. Now wasn't the time to tell her, but I needed to pass on the Soapies.

Gunter carried Poppy's knuckles to his mouth and kissed them suavely. "I am grateful for your company. You ah beautiful both outside and in."

Poppy wiggled happily. "I know, right?"

Gun met my eyes and winked cheekily as if I were part of some hilarious inside joke. I nearly flipped him off—I wouldn't laugh at Poppy's expense—until I realized the joke was on him. I wouldn't laugh at Gun either. "I'm glad you had a nice time. I need to check the bar."

"Wait." Poppy touched my sleeve. "Joey said to tell you to call him—where's your phone?"

"It's still dead. It's on my to-do list for tomorrow."

"Okay—well he thinks you can get some kind of settlement for the car thing, because of your injury. Did you see a doctor?"

"I'm about to."

"Good. As your partner and as your friend—go to the fucking doctor. Oh. Joey says to tell you the air bag shouldn't have deployed. He thinks Crappy's tampered with it."

"Cappy's."

"Same difference. He says to tell you he's on it, and you're going to get some money. Hot damn!" Her avarice had Gunter even more enthralled. He trapped her again in his double-pawed actor clutch and I glared at their clasped hands. Poppy said, "Call Joey first thing."

"Will do."

"Promise?"

"Yup."

Gunter looked between us both. "It is astounding to me that Shep is blessed with such good people in his life."

"I'm stuck with him..." Poppy sighed, "...forever."

"Then I am too," I said.

Shep and Gunter stationed themselves in the elegant foyer with sprightly Poppy nestled between them as the rest of us cleaned, ran dishes, packed booze and broke down the bar. I had Vito distribute plates of leftovers to the paparazzi and the security team. They were on the street eating skewered salmon puffs and roasted beet crostini. As feeding people is part of my heritage, I felt better in spirit.

At last, my uncles brought the van around, then they hugged me, foraged for a few cigars from Shep's stash and left to take the subway home.

Dan hovered. "Are you sure—?"

"Yes. Go handle your thing."

"I'd rather you handle it for me."

"Funny, but I'm not in the mood. Just go do whatever it is—secure the perimeter? Reconnaissance? Peep. Lurk. I'll be back in forty minutes and then I'm going to sleep."

"Take a cab. No subway."

"Cab?" I balked. The ghost of my penny-pinching grandfather lectured inside my memory. "But that's so extravagant."

"Take. A. Cab. They are yellow and it'll cost you five bucks. Hail one, you hear me, Romano? Maybe you'll get lucky and the *Cash Cab* will pick you up."

"Oh. I'd like that, actually."

He shook his head.

Shep sauntered in and hugged me with one arm while I winced. "Thanks, Ce. This was great. I know it was difficult—and it was short notice—but I really appreciate it."

"Sure. I think Gun was a real hit."

Shep ignored that and said, "Vito and Tino were fantastic. They said *forget-about-it* and waved their hands around and stole all my cigars. Everyone loved them. You know, sometimes I forget how much I liked your family."

"I asked them to do that for you."

"I only wish Jean Luc could have been here," he said sadly.

"Well...it would have made the evening...extra special for me too."

And that was it. I was done. Sort of a let down after three intense days, but *Holy Mother of Mary* was I glad it was over. Dan pecked my cheek, I picked up the bag of linens, promptly deposited them back on the floor—that could wait—and Stephen Taylor, his iPhone and I headed to the street.

Naturally Jorge Carrera waited for me at side door. I just...couldn't deal with him. For once he was straggly, having waited outside in the humidity all evening. Heat lightning flashed across the moonless sky as I handed Jorge a Posh Nosh business card. "Can you just call me tomorrow? I'm not well, but I may have something for you."

Jorge stared at the card like I'd given him a wedding ring. "Yes. Sure. I'm doing a big piece on celebrities' employees—you'd be perfect for this. Thanks, Caesar."

"That sounds..." *Galling.* "...interesting."

Behind Shep's building, it was black as pitch, but around the corner, 57th Street was lit with streetlights and apartment buildings and passing vehicles. The bang of a car door closing and laughter on the sidewalks drifted into the alley. A clap of thunder drowned everything as we climbed into the van. I wrestled my seat belt over my chest, and then I unhooked it. No way. No *fucking* way was I tightening that vise across my body.

"There's no air, so roll your window down" was all the conversation I wanted to have with the brisk, young assistant seated beside me. How had I come to such a state as this? I was ferrying Stephen Taylor home. I punched the gas, pain shooting all the way to my groin, and we puttered slowly onto the street.

Off-duty, Stephen turned into a regular Chatty Cathy. Away from his boss and free of weighty responsibility, he tapped on his iPhone and yakked without taking a breath. "So. I wonder who's going to win tomorrow. I hope it's Shep, but if it's Gunter that's okay too."

"I wouldn't know—"

"What's the deal with Gunter? Did he come on to you? He flirts with anyone who walks through the door, but he won't look at me. It's like he doesn't really *see* me, you know? Like I'm invisible. But who cares? He's so gorgeous. His eyes are the color of new leaves in spring. And his accent? It just melts my cheese."

"Cheese? That's a bit...hearty." I gripped the wheel and turned wide enough to steer our ship downtown. Horns blasted behind me. The city lights twinkled in every direction, but above us, the blackened sky boiled with fast-moving clouds.

It was going to rain buckets any minute now. At last, cool air came through the open window. I tried to return some small talk. What had he said? "The longer you're around actors, the more immune you become to their charms. Trust me. Gunter's flirtatious. He doesn't mean anything by it—he flirts with everyone. It's like...practice. I think they take classes in that."

"Well, he doesn't flirt with me. I try. I'm cute. I pay attention to style. I'm way younger than you and he flirts with you all the time. He just pats my hand and coos at me like I'm twelve." Stephen sulked.

I slanted a look at my passenger. He was twenty-two and a fresh faced twink-in-the-city—I'd been that young once, as he happily reminded me, the little prick. When I was his age, I'd worn that charmingly stupid mustache. "Look, Stephen. Gunter's a good guy—but you're an employee and...and...well...uh...he's not the type...you know...to—"

"Oh whatever." He waved his hand around. "Caesar. Mr. Romano. I don't even know what to call you...and *hello!* What is with your uncles? Are they for real? I'm sorry we got off on the wrong foot. I try to be very proper for Mr. McNamara—he's paying me a lot of money. I want to keep my job. You used to go with him, right? I can't see that. I feel like, if I'm not uber professional, that Jean Luc guy will do something nasty in front of me."

"Good call."

"And since my aunt Estelle got me this job, I have to make a perfect impression."

"Estelle Rosenstein is your aunt?"

"Yes. I'm half Jewish on my mother's side. Anyway. You should know this. I have this...problem when I'm under a lot of stress. I have a bad memory for faces. Really bad. Like it's *clinical.* Usually I take someone's photo sort of when they're not looking and I label it with their names, right? And then when I'm on the subway, I practice remembering. Like flashcards. I have an app for that."

"App?" That's why he was in tears when I broke his phone. I was speechless until I hit a rut in the road and that stupid yelp/gasp noise slipped from my lips as my lung seized.

"Did you just hit a dog?" Stephen looked in the rearview mirror and then he craned around to peer through the back door.

"I don't know. Maybe." I gasped.

A transformer buzzed on the street as Stephen slumped forward. I waited until I caught my breath. "Uhm. Are you okay?" He jerked once. "Was that a yes or a no? Did you drop something on the floor? Your phone?"

"No. He's out."

Fear lifted my ass a good six inches off the driver's seat. My foot slipped from the gas and the van swerved into the other lane. Pain shot through my shoulders as I fought to get the damn truck on track. We narrowly missed colliding with a cab, who wasted no time swerving back at me. "*Fuck!*"

"Keep your eyes on the road, Mister."

I gripped the wheel with both hands, ten and two position, and stared in open confusion at the angry dark-haired child in my rearview mirror. I turned. There was a Girl Scout in my vehicle. *A scout.* She had a sash covered in colorful badges and pins and a little white shirt with a Peter Pan collar. "Isn't it past your bedtime? Where's your mother?"

"I said, eyes on the road, douchebag."

I spun around. "Mind your manners. That was totally uncalled for. Are you lost?"

I glanced out the window, wondering if Child Protective Services was searching for this wayward child, and Stephen's hand flopped onto my thigh. He was coming around. "Wha? Wha?"

"Shut up, Stephen. Just go to sleep." The Girl Scout pressed something against his arm, and the inside of the van crackled as if four hundred thousand volts of electricity had been released with the press of a trigger. Stephen jerked, then he slumped again.

Terror turned the inside of my mouth to ash. "*Kendal?*"

Her stun gun was like something straight from Dr. Frankenstein's laboratory.

"That's me, dickweed. You need to turn this pussy wagon around."

"I beg your pardon?"

"I can't believe that Poppy chick makes you drive a pink van."

"I can't believe you're a furry." That slipped out before I could catch it, but she was vile. How had Gunter stomached this girl? Not just...you know...*sex*...but in principle.

The first fat drop of water hit the windshield and a gust of wind blew a newspaper across the intersection. The streets were alive with swift-moving cabs—taillights glowing in the now-falling rain—and pedestrians ran for cover as the clouds finally followed through on their threat. One minute it was clear, the next a deluge of water poured from the heavens.

Inside the van, it was tight with tension. I fumbled for the wipers.

"I'm not a furry. Lester is a furry—and so are his friends. I was a seamstress and he just...worships me. You can imagine that a girl who can sew an anatomically correct chipmunk makes him especially committed. Now, shut up and turn the fucking van around."

Kendal Schmidt was armed, in my van, and no one in a million years would take her for anything but a foul-mouthed child. She had braids that were tied with *bows*. She was an adorable freckle-faced little girl with a sewing badge and a community-service pin and a beanie. She was a sociopathic Girl Scout parading around in knee socks, who could kill me and stand on the corner skipping rope while the police outlined my cold body with chalk ten feet away and no one would look twice at her. They'd buy her cookies.

I was getting a little ahead of myself, but Kendal Schmidt turned hiding in plain sight into an art form.

"Did you hear me, Romano, turn the van around."

"Okay. Okay. Calm down. I need to go around the block."

"You're going to take me into the apartment. You dig? I'm going to fry Gunter's dick, and then I'm going to cook his nuts until they smoke."

Wow. She was tough as well as incredibly specific. She waved her stun gun around, and my stomach turned.

"I'm not really a fan of violence." I put my blinker on and eased the van onto a side street. "Why are you obsessed with terrifying Gun? This is pointless. You knew what you were getting into. You signed a waiver, for Christ's sake."

"Because Lester never made a pass at anyone—Gunter made that up. Gunter fired me for *personal reasons*," she spat. "He didn't like me."

"Can you blame him? You're a little high-strung. What did you expect?"

"You have no idea the things he said to me." Her voice pitched higher. "He...said he loved me."

"Oh, for pity's sake, this is all about being a woman scorned? Way to live up to a stereotype."

"Just shut the fuck up and drive. I like your little pink tie. Very studly," she said nastily.

Sharp droplets of rain pinged through the open window, and I had to work the crank to close it. Each jerk of my hand sent another fit of discomfort to my torso. Stephen was getting soaked. Kendal yanked him from his seat and let him fall on the floor.

This was my opportunity to do something heroic and

masculine, but I had neither the endurance nor the agility, and I was lacking even the most rudimentary plan.

"Where's your cell phone?"

I thought she was asking Stephen so I kept mum.

Something cold pressed against my neck and I recoiled. Kendal said harshly, "Answer me, Caesar. Where is your cell phone?"

"I...it's dead. I dropped it this morning on $4^{th}$ Street."

She slid into the passenger seat and closed the window. Her uniform turned out to be one of those old-fashioned green dress types. She was a very retro scout. She had Buster Browns on her feet and if she'd worn that clubbing, she'd have made a big splash.

We were four blocks from Shep's when I came to a careful, controlled halt at the traffic light. What the hell was her goal? I mean, other than roasting Gunter's nuts. She couldn't zap me and still get what she wanted. She also couldn't zap me while I was driving. I could just...let her zap me? Maybe Dan would save the day as Kendal tried to enter the fortified building—there's no way she could get in without me. She must know that.

Lightning flashed behind me, which was odd until I realized the car behind me had hit the high beams.

"Uh...why—?"

"Shut up. Just don't talk. No more talking." She rubbed her hand against her jittery leg, so agitated I zipped my trap.

The windshield wipers slapped and rain sluiced off the roof, and I fumbled for the defroster. Fog coated the windows. I wiped the driver's door window with my hand, and the white Camry pulled beside me at the traffic light.

I blinked. Yup. Still there.

Where the hell had he come from? The answer was pretty clear. He was following me. Again. No, he followed me always. What had he said? *Maybe I should just follow you 24/7.*

Kendal spat, "Just drive, *paesan*, and when we get there pull into the alley. Don't do anything stupid."

The light changed and I punched the gas, my left foot valiantly working the clutch. I needed to do something rash to throw her off-guard and signal Dan, but for the first time all week nothing remotely impulsive came to mind. Maybe the Motrin had dulled my wits.

Dan pulled through the intersection, and I politely gave him the room he needed to cut in front of me. Could I flash the lights? Beep the horn? Rear-end him? As God was my witness, *no more accidents*. Kendal's hand on the wicked stun gun was threat enough to drive slow and careful.

I needed to do something out of character, so I pushed the accelerator, giving the van as much juice as it had. It wasn't much—nothing like the Camry's speed. I accelerated until my foot was on the floor and we were inches from Dan's bumper. Kendal rubbed her thigh and bit at her lips—she was a twitchy girl—but she didn't notice my erratic driving. To her mind, I was a typical New York driver.

"C'mon, Nana's boy, go around this asshole."

My foot slipped again and we slowed. "You *bitch*. That was you? *You were in my house last night?*"

"Yes," she said testily. "So what? I tried to do this last night, but between Lester moping after me constantly, and then your satanic cat, it didn't happen."

"Why would you do that? *That's my grandmother's house.*" My voice bounced through the truck—I'm surprised I didn't wake Stephen.

"I need you to get in the door. You're so...hooked in to these people. I never heard of you until yesterday and *bam*, Caesar Romano, everywhere I went. I thought maybe Gunter hired a private investigator. You were in my apartment. Mrs. Rousseau told me you were there with some cop and you were too quiet. She said you were FBI."

"Me? She's a lunatic." Obviously, Kendal didn't know about Dan—Mr. Flies-Under-The-Radar.

"I still think this is a cover. I tried to call Stephen, and every time I asked him who you were..."

"He didn't know."

"He doesn't know who *I* am either. He's such an idiot."

I gained on the Camry, and then, without using a blinker, I changed lanes. Sweat broke on my lip as I went around the car. I'd just passed illegally. I mopped my forehead with my sleeve and soldiered on.

Ahead, at the intersection, the light turned yellow and...

I stomped the gas. I gave Poppy's van everything it had, and as the light turned red, I barreled through the intersection and ran the light. My heart slammed against my battered ribs. I hadn't driven like this since...well since that incident a few weeks ago.

The van careened along and I wove through traffic like I had something offensive to prove.

A blue light flashed behind us. Kendal said, "Slow down. Let him pass or I'll fry him like an egg, you hear me?" She placed her weapon on Stephen's neck, and I nodded and eased us through traffic. The blue light flared, and then the cruiser took a left and disappeared into the rain.

I stopped at the light. The rain pissed down, bouncing on the now-clear sidewalks, and ran in a current to the storm drains. My door jerked open and Dan's big, scarred hand reached into the van, and he dragged me onto the street like he was hauling a giant marlin onto the deck of his Uncle Riley's sport fishing boat.

"Shit." I shrieked and it wasn't pretty. Dan literally tossed me onto the filthy street, and I flopped onto the ground, blinded by the Camry's headlights. I knew he was saving me, but Jesus, I was soaked from above and below. He'd deposited me in a puddle, on 6th Avenue, New York, NY. Every known germ in America crawled onto my skin.

A car door slammed and wet feet slapped the pavement from the other side of the van. Dan took off. I'd drown if I laid here another second—or catch syphilis—so using the van, I climbed to my knees.

Dan hollered above the storm, but I couldn't hear him. He was a wet blur in the downpour, his strong legs eating the sidewalk as he chased the diminutive Girl Scout. She circled cars and ran behind trucks, putting every effort into keeping free of Dan's clutches. They moved toward the subway.

Stephen staggered into the driver's seat. "What? Were we in an accident? I can't remember—"

"Give me your phone—no, call the apartment. Tell Gun to get the police. Tell him right now."

Stephen nodded shakily.

"Take the van." I barked orders and Stephen's head pivoted loosely on his neck. "Shit. Do you even know who I am?"

"You're Caesar. Check. I'll call the apartment and tell them...tell them...what?"

"Just call 9-1-1."

I hobbled to the Camry. We'd stopped traffic behind us and—thank you, NYPD—help was on its way. Blue light and sirens approached from the east—I should have known Dan would have it covered. I jumped into the Camry, and regardless of the pain and the stench and the dozens of twirling Christmas trees, I took the corner, leaving the traffic behind me. I headed after Dan and Kendal.

She was fast, that little scrapper. She was armed, she looked like a drowned-rat nine-year-old, and none of that stopped Dan. Kendal ran flat out, her little legs pedaling. She shed her costume as she raced for the subway. She lost her beanie, her sash, her hair bows. I hoped she wouldn't strip her shirt.

I braked at the subway stop, and Kendal flew past just as Dan launched himself into the air like flipping Batman. He had power and speed and damn good aim. He also had about two hundred pounds of muscle mass. He brought Kendal Schmidt to the concrete easily, and I don't think he bothered to break her fall.

"*She's got a taser!*"

With one hand he slammed her wrist, and her weapon tumbled into the gutter. Damn. He was every kind of kick ass.

Of course, she was four-eleven, but nonetheless, I was impressed.

By midnight I'd given my statement. I was in the emergency room, floating comfortably toward the ceiling under the influence of doctor-prescribed happy pills when Gunter and Dan came through the door. They'd finished with the police. The two found me lolling on a gurney, dressed in my sexy blue-checkered hospital gown. It was easy access if nothing else. I smiled stupidly at the thought.

Gun was still in his suit from the party—minus the jacket. His sleeves were rolled to the elbow, the tie was gone, and his shirt opened to his chest. His sandy hair was still slicked back, and he looked like a beautiful but world-weary lawyer from a crime drama. I was high enough to believe a stylist prepared him before he entered. No matter how you sliced it, he was a beautiful man.

Dan looked rough—not just tired and crabby, but like a hot, mean dockworker. Someone had loaned him a navy blue T-shirt and a pair of faded jeans. He glared at my chart like he wanted to speak with someone about my quality of care.

Bless him, he also held a takeout bag.

I smiled from my narcotic haze and said dreamily, "Hey."

Naturally Dan kissed my cheek and then he collapsed into the cheap plastic chair in the corner. He hooked his feet on the rail of my bed and rolled me his way. He said, "That's done," as if I should tick it off our to-do list or something.

"That chick was a handful." I eyed Gun and tried to say something positive about Kendal, for his sake, but I had nothing except, "She could run very fast."

Dan opened the bag and handed me a pink donut and a napkin. He admitted, "I never would have recognized her. She looked like she was selling cookies."

Gunter said stiffly, "She is unpleasant at the best of times—but I want to make it clear she always dressed as an adult when we were together."

"That's a good thing," I said around a mouthful of strawberry frosting.

"The last year has been difficult, very lonely, you understand?"

"You could have had the pick of the boys…"

"Yes. And if you could have the pick of the girls, how would that be for you?"

I shuddered delicately around my mouthful of donut.

"Touché. But Kendal?"

"After my arrest for solicitation—"

"But...but that was a man."

Gunter flushed to his sculpted hairline. "I...he was dressed as a woman. I truly thought he was a she."

"Well, that happens to the best of us," I said.

Dan snorted in agreement.

"After the incident, I resorted to an indiscretion with someone unstable, unsuitable and as I found out later, involved in something...unsavory. She was, however, convenient and willing. I am forever paying for my lack of judgment with more lack of judgment."

"Blech. Self-pity doesn't suit you at all," I said.

Dan snickered and said to me, "I still can't believe you were almost felled by a Girl Scout."

"She had a weapon and I'm injured and *you're fucking welcome* for finding her for you again, *Detective*."

Gunter changed the subject, and who could blame him? "I wanted to thank you for everything. You ah as interesting and naughty as I suspected." He parked his cute ass on the gurney and kissed my cheek—*kiss kiss*—and then he hugged me with care. "You ah well, *Schatz*?"

"I am, but no more BMWs for me."

Dan watched Gun, but he grumbled to me, "You have your prescription?"

"That I do." I fluttered my paper at him. "I can go as soon as you help me put on my pants."

Gunter wasn't finished. "Before we part, I wanted to apologize to you for this ruse, Caesar. I know it makes you uncomfortable."

"It does—but we all make stupid mistakes when we're twenty. It's how we deal with the consequences that matter. You find a girlfriend, preferably not a psychotic redhead, and live your life, Gun. You deserve to be happy."

"I would do that. It is tricky, of course. I don't want to upset or anger the people I care for—the people who haff supported me."

"The alternative is allowing people like Kendal to have control over you," Dan said.

"I know. We make such bad choices—if only mine were as simple to fix as the bad mustache, yes?"

"Oh, I made worse mistakes than that," I added cheerfully.

Dan muttered, "Yes and we see Shep by the day."

Gun continued, "I would fire Estelle but it solves nothing."

I had a thought—a drug-induced thought, but I shared it anyway. "Do the same thing you did when you were twenty-two. Don't announce it—just do it. Get a girlfriend. No biggie."

Dan stopped mid search for my pants. "He's right. I think that's the only way. It could be that easy."

"Sometimes it is." I smiled.

"This is a blessing, yes? I have so few people I call friends, but I would be honored to have you both as my friends."

Dan shrugged. "As long as your check clears, you keep your hands off my boyfriend, and you buy the first round, we're cool."

My laugh was cut short. "No joking. It hurts to laugh."

"Who said I was joking?"

Gun stood. "As long as the first round is nonalcoholic, then yes."

"So, who do you think will win tomorrow night?" I wasn't

going to put my pants on without assistance and Dan seemed to know that. He stood to help me.

"C'mon, Ce. Shake a leg." His words in no way matched his actions.

"You haff to ask? Me. I am the better actor. You will see. Shep is all style and no substance."

"Are you sure you don't like men just a little?" I was half joking. "They're much more fun. I promise."

Gun moved close, taking my hand, and he leaned to whisper, "Maybe for you, luff."

"Give it a rest, Heidelbach."

He gave me a broad wink before teasing Dan. "You ah such the boyfriend, Albright. Very much in luff, ah you not?"

"You better believe it."

Either these drugs were better than I imagined, or Dan had just admitted he loved me. I snuck him a look, and he nodded. *Wow.* These were *damn* good drugs.

Gun finger-combed his hair, and with another *kiss kiss* he headed for the door.

I had to know. "What are you going to do?"

"Now I am going to speak with my publicist, find a date for tomorrow night and let Kendal tell her story. And as you say, no one will belief I had sex with that woman. She is vile."

"I can scarcely believe it. You can do so much better, but keep your paws off Poppy."

"You haf my word."

# Epilogue

Dan Albright came in from his homey kitchen juggling two piping hot plates of veal scallopini. With one foot, he dragged the coffee table closer to my cushy nest on his big comfortable couch. We were in Staten Island, in the small home he'd inherited from his grandparents when they'd packed their library and their collection of family photos and moved to Scottsdale to better enjoy their golden years. Behind me, the picture window faced a tree-lined street straight out of Mayberry, and nearby, the campus of Wagner College lit the hillside. Manhattan glowed across the river.

It was Saturday night and by some miraculous twist of fate—a cracked rib—I was watching the *26th Annual Soapie Awards* from Staten Island, instead of attending at Radio City. Beautiful, happy people filled the flat screen, and I eased against the couch pillows, delightfully tipsy with relief.

Dan set our plates on the glass surface.

"Hey. Why's my food so far away?"

"Let it cool. If you burn your lips, what's left of my love life is over."

I chuckled and it hurt. "Shut up. Don't make me laugh."

He settled beside me and reached for his beer. "Are you disappointed we didn't go?"

"Are you kidding me? Not at all. I'm relieved. Besides, Joey needs to spend this time with Poppy. They're a family now. It would behoove them to act like one." My throat tightened a little. They were a family—and soon, they'd be married.

The camera zoomed in and we saw the scarlet-clad Poppy McNamara (cousin to award nominee for best actor in a daytime drama and star of *Mr. Potter's Lullaby*, Sundays this summer at 8 on NBC, Sheppard McNamara) again. That was six times—we were keeping track of our Poppy sightings.

Dan picked at the wet beer label with a thumbnail and nodded toward the TV. "You're sure you're not disappointed?"

I stared at him. He watched the television, his face clean of expression and I knew—it mattered to him. "You wanted to go. Why didn't you say something? Are *you* disappointed?"

"Not exactly. Shep's safe—I'm not thrilled to pay someone else to keep an eye on him, but had we gone, I sort of wanted to see you in that tux again. Maybe take a whirl on the dance floor, like we said. We should do that."

"We should. Let's do it right here." I tossed the covers and tried to stand. Before I ever made it to my feet Dan latched onto the back of my sweats.

"Whoa there, Jack. Where do you think you're going? Rest. Doctor's orders. You're medicated."

"Oh, simmer down, Nurse Betty. I'm only going upstairs for a second."

I left him on the couch worrying the inside of his cheek and nursing his beer. Our food cooled on the table, but as I climbed the narrow stairs to Dan's bedroom, his fork clinked on the plate.

Unlike Nana's house, the upstairs light burned frivolously. I passed the spare rooms on the way to Dan's modest bedroom at the end of the hall. Inside, the walls and trim were rich browns and deep blues. The furnishings were heavy and bold, and the bedding was plain and comfortable and rumpled to hell. It was undeniably masculine here, and it suited him.

I found what I was looking for, but stopped in front of the old marble-topped dresser. Dan had a photograph of his grandparents taken on the steps of this house. He had one of him and his cousin on the back of his uncle's boat. They were dressed in ugly vests and held dead silvery fish. He had one more photo. This one taken the day I started my new job at Posh Nosh—I was eating a cupcake.

I slid open the top drawer. Inside, my clothes were neatly tucked away—a few shirts, a couple pair of jeans, some underwear. I was here for at least the short run—and the long haul if we were lucky. He'd cleared a drawer for me this morning with a stern look at my bandage and a squeeze of his hand on mine.

That damn lump was back in my throat—because I'd missed something vital. Dan was into romantic gestures far more than I was. Which meant he needed romance far more than I did. I could give him that—Caesar Romano style. I wouldn't roll my eyes either, but only because for him, I'd mean it.

*Shit.* He loved me.

Downstairs, Dan sneaked a forkful of veal cutlet. He took a guilty look at me hobbling around the banister, and his hand froze halfway between plate and mouth. His jaw dropped. "Holy hell, Caesar, what are you doing?"

"I know, right? This is the single nicest article of clothing I've ever seen, never mind owned, so lose the fork, big guy, before you get marinara everywhere. Here. Put this on."

"You're insane, you know that?" But he shrugged into his

dinner jacket, and I turned the volume down on the television.

"Okay. You wait here. I'll be right back." I smoothed my hand over my satin lapels. "Oh. Move the furniture. I can't do that."

He muttered, "Give a man an inch..." as I went into the office.

The workspace took half the square footage of the first floor. I flipped the light and dug through his disorganized collection of CDs—he really needed to do something with this. Alphabetize at the very least. I could buy some bins and bring my label maker from Nan's and really set this place straight. I had sharpies and paperclips, and I was nearly erect thinking about organizing the office.

Back in the living room, Dan stood silhouetted at the window, staring at the flickering TV. His black formal wear was perfectly contrasted by red plaid pajama bottoms and a chiseled chest. Hair swirled across his pecs—his scars hidden under the jacket. The coffee table and the leather recliner were shoved against the far wall. Dan watched the award ceremony, sipping beer and tapping the remote against his thigh.

I cleared my throat, and he looked at me and frowned. "This is crazy."

"No. It's romantic."

"Since when is Caesar Romano ever romantic?"

"Since never. No. Since you." I loaded the CD player and pressed play. "So, how do we do this?"

His eyebrows arched when the music started, but he had no trouble dictating how this was going to go. "I lead. You follow. Seems straightforward enough." Brown eyes twinkled and my heart lurched.

"That doesn't sound fair, does it? I think you're taking

advantage."

"I'm taller. I can see where we're going. I'm older and wiser. I lead. You follow. That's how it's done, baby." He took my hands in his.

"I have to dance backwards? You mean I'm working harder? That does sound par for the course."

Dan slid his arm under mine, and he drew me close until our chests touched. "I promise, I won't let you fall."

His left hand came to rest light and firm, but high on my back. I placed one palm on his shoulder, my fingers holding him gently, and the other palm I laid into his outstretched hand.

"What the hell is this?"

"Just go with it, Albright. It's Chris Brown. I didn't think your Bruce Springsteen collection was appropriate."

He moved left. I did too and he stumbled over my feet. "Your big Italian feet are in the way." But he caught me softly—so I wouldn't strain anything—and we found a rhythm, swaying together in the small living room.

"This is about the gayest thing I've ever done in my life."

"Somehow, I sincerely doubt that."

He held me, it felt like forever, until the song ended and I rested my cheek on his. On the big screen, Gunter Heidelbach, the most deserving actor ever to appear on daytime television, rose to his feet and adjusted his cuffs. He grinned, green eyes laughing and, winking into the camera, he made his way to the podium.

# About the Author

LB Gregg began writing in the spring of 2008 at the encouragement of author pal, Josh Lanyon. She never once looked back (although occasionally she looked down and tripped over her own feet). 2009 saw the publication of her best selling Men of Smithfield series.

LB lives in the Connecticut hills with two lazy dogs, three above-average children, and a smoking hot husband who, thank the good Lord, loves to cook.

You can find LB at her blog, Noseinabook: http://lisabea.blogspot.com or visit her website www.lbgregg.com.

*The fear of getting caught is half the fun.*

# Catch Me If You Can

## *© 2010 LB Gregg*

*Romano and Albright, Book 1*

Lowly art gallery assistant Caesar Romano is freely out of the closet. Now he'd just like to get out of his Nana's guest room. Everything—his reputation and his financial freedom—is riding on the success of tonight's gallery opening. If only he could shake free of the past so easily.

A mysterious gatecrasher, Dan Green, looks like a promising addition to his pending new life—until Caesar's ex shows up and suddenly the opening disintegrates into a half-naked dance melee. When the glitter settles, a missing sculpture of Justin Timberlake has Caesar up to his eyebrows in extortion, intrigue and a wild sexual adventure underneath, inside, and on top of a variety of furnishings.

As the cast of suspects piles up, so do the questions. Like who's really blackmailing whom? And what does a stolen paint-by-numbers clown matter when Dan is so outrageously capable of blowing Caesar's resistance to smithereens?

*Warning: This book contains graphic language, sex, lies, intrigue, clowns, kleptomania, anal sex, oral sex, mutual masturbation, bad driving, good cooking, and the missing head of a Justin Timberlake statue. Not for the sour of disposition.*

*What the tide washes in, the past can sweep away.*

# Driftwood

## *© 2010 Harper Fox*

All Dr. Tom Penrose wants is his old life back. He's home in Cornwall after a hellish tour of duty in Afghanistan, but while the village is the same, he isn't. His grip on his control is fragile, and it slips dangerously when Flynn Summers explodes into his life. The vision in tight neoprene nearly wipes them both out in a surfing mishap—and shatters Tom's lonely peace.

Flynn is a crash-and-burn in progress, one of only two survivors of a devastating rescue helicopter crash that killed his crew. His carefree charm is merely a cover for the messed-up soul within. The sparks between him and Tom are the first light he's seen in a long, dark tunnel of self-recrimination, which includes living in sexual thrall to fellow crash survivor and former co-pilot, Robert.

As their attraction burns through spring and into summer, Tom must confront not only his own shadows, but Flynn's—before the past rises up to swallow his lover whole.

*Warning: Contains explicit m/m sex, hot helicopter pilots and skin-tight wetsuits. Also, in true British tradition, a tiny bit of joystick innuendo.*

CPSIA information can be obtained at www.ICGtesting.com
Printed in the USA
LVOW111601101111
254403LV00005B/44/P